THE RED QUEEN RULES

**The Red Solaris Mystery Series
by Bourne Morris**

THE RED QUEEN'S RUN (#1)
THE RISE OF THE RED QUEEN (#2)
THE RED QUEEN RULES (#3)

THE RED QUEEN RULES (#3)

"Morris hits it out of the park...It is smart, fast-paced, and utterly contemporary with plot lines of disturbing hate groups and higher education's attempts to teach students how to respond peacefully yet effectively to hate speech."

– Don Hardy,
Author of *Because I'd Just Hate to Disappear*

"Once again, the inquisitive and impulsive Red Solaris ricochets between ivory tower abstractions and real world mayhem. The best Red Queen mystery yet."

– Ann Ronald,
Author of *Friendly Fallout 1953*

"Red Solaris is intelligent, tough, and vulnerable, a tricky combination to pull off, yet Bourne Morris does so beautifully and has given us a lead character we care deeply about."

– Annette Dashofy,
USA Today Bestselling Author of *With a Vengeance*

THE RISE OF THE RED QUEEN (#2)

"With *The Rise of the Red Queen*, Bourne Morris is poised to become the queen of academic mysteries and suspense."

– Gigi Pandian,
USA Today Bestselling Author of *Quicksand*

"Intriguing characters, a complex, inventive plot with nail-biting suspense—I finished it at two in the morning!"

– Jeanne M. Dams,
Author of the Dorothy Martin Mysteries

"Morris has written another delicious pleasure, providing intrigue, plenty of campus drama, and strong female characters. Academic in-fighting, Red's ambition to become the new Dean, and her detective love interest keep the pages turning."

– Karen Penner-Johnson,
Emerita Professor, Kansas State University

"The story involved me quickly, the suspense mounting so high that when my e-reader battery ran low, the warning buzzer made me jump. Morris has created a complete mystery with suspense and emotions burning like a Nevada sunset."

– Mark Bacon,
Author of *Death in Nostalgia City*

THE RED QUEEN'S RUN (#1)

"Touching upon a very real subject, this author offers the perfect formula of suspects, mystery, and a handsome police detective to heat up Red's fire...a great read about what goes on behind those academic doors."

– *Suspense Magazine*

"Morris has crafted a suspenseful, thoughtful, sexy debut...Her hero, Red Solaris, is vulnerable but tough, complex but straight-shooting, a woman learning how to wield power by remembering what it's like to have little of it...Long live the Queen!"

– Christopher Coake,
Author of *You Came Back*

"Morris proves herself a masterful storyteller in this compelling debut novel. *The Red Queen's Run* is compulsive reading as it takes on the ripped-from-the-headlines topic of campus violence. I can't wait to follow its smart new heroine."

– Alan Deutschman,
Author of *Change or Die*

THE RED QUEEN RULES

A Red Solaris Mystery

Bourne Morris

HENERY PRESS

THE RED QUEEN RULES
A Red Solaris Mystery
Part of the Henery Press Mystery Collection

First Edition | December 2016

Henery Press
www.henerypress.com

Trade Paperback ISBN-13: 978-1-63511-121-7
Digital epub ISBN-13: 978-1-63511-122-4
Kindle ISBN-13: 978-1-63511-123-1
Hardcover Paperback ISBN-13: 978-1-63511-124-8

Printed in the United States of America

For my grandchildren.
May they forever enjoy freedom of speech.

ACKNOWLEDGMENTS

Little did I know when I started writing my first mystery that it would turn into three books. But my wonderfully supportive agent, Kimberley Cameron, believed that the story of Red Solaris had the legs to run through a full trilogy so I kept going. I am forever indebted to her.

Several helpful and long-suffering readers also deserve thanks and praise. For this third book, a special salute to Cecelia Pearce, as always, and Mark Bacon, a wonderful writer who took time out from his own work to help with mine.

As usual, I counted on editors, Anna Davis, Erin George and Rachel Jackson at Henery Press to make the book better. They never fail me.

More applause should go to reviewers. Ann Ronald has won awards for her books on the West. Don Hardy's recent creation is a compelling blog on his fight against cancer. They are distinguished academics with intellects and writing talents superior to mine and, fortunately, they share my taste for murder and mystery.

Holly Austin Smith, author of Walking Prey; How America's Youth are Vulnerable to Sex Slavery, taught me what young girls endure when trapped in this crime, and Sergeant Ron Chalmers described the reality of the Reno, Nevada Police Department's war on the sex trade in Nevada. I greatly admire the Reno PD and others who work to help save the children and women in my hometown. I hope they will accept my apologies for indulging in exaggerations for dramatic effect. Any errors in describing police work are entirely my own.

Carla B. Higginbotham, Assistant US Attorney, District of Nevada, first alerted me to the magnitude of the problem in this state with her articulate and fact-filled presentation on sex trafficking in Nevada and America.

I am blessed with a group of amazing friends who critique and encourage and keep me sane. So do some wonderful book clubs and Sundance, the best of all possible bookstores.

Finally, daughters Miranda and Temple, and stepson Scott, cheer me on, and my dear husband, Bob, keeps me happily writing and grateful to be living with him.

Chapter 1

The shouting came from somewhere east of the parking lot. It was dark and cold and I was exhausted after a twelve-hour workday. I wanted to get home to Joe and hot food. But the shouts were not the boisterous noises of college students who'd had too much to drink. No laughter. No celebration. Instead the sound of an angry man bellowing. A sharp sense of impending violence cut through the night air. A momentary lull was followed by a woman's voice, higher than the rest.

"You bastards, I have every right to be here."

I knew her voice and instinctively ran toward the sound.

Porch lights illuminated a group on the front lawn of a large white house. The house belonged to a fringe student organization of white supremacists who called themselves The American Purists. On our campus, The Purists were a small group who usually went ignored when they weren't being derided.

They were noted primarily for posters proclaiming beliefs so extreme they could easily be mistaken for satire. The posters would go up in the early morning and, usually by nightfall, would be covered with epithets written by other students who referred to the Purists as nut-wings, "neither left-wing nor right-wing, just somewhere totally off the grid."

No one on the faculty or in the rest of the student body took the Purists seriously. Once in a while, some graffiti would appear on the side of the large white Victorian house the Purists occupied, but for the most part they were left to themselves.

But that night they were out in force, at least ten of them surrounding a slender girl who lay on the edge of the lawn. A smashed cell phone lay beside her.

"No right to take photographs," growled one of the young men, crouching down near the girl's head.

"Get out of here," said a tall girl standing beside him. "Or you're going to get hurt."

The prone girl rolled over and struggled to her feet, taking two steps back onto the sidewalk in front of the house. She was smaller and shorter than the others. "I just wanted to get a shot of them," she said, pointing to figures standing several yards away in front of a partially constructed platform at the side of the house. I could just make them out, two men and a woman, their faces in the shadow of the house.

The tall girl took a step toward her and stomped on the lifeless cell phone. "No pictures, bitch. Leave."

But the smaller girl stood her ground. Even in the inadequate light from the porch her posture showed defiance. "You assholes should welcome the publicity. Or do you think the local papers are really going to cover your extremist guest speaker? She'll be on page seven at the bottom."

"Leave. Now." The tall girl took a step closer.

"That'll be enough," I said, moving into the light. The group came out of its knot. Several headed back to the house, leaving the tall girl and her growling companion on the lawn.

"Get your reporter out of here," said the boy, looking slightly nervous and less belligerent than before.

I turned to the defiant girl on the sidewalk. "Rosie, go home. It's late. We'll talk about this in the morning."

"Dammit, Red. They broke my phone. It cost me a couple hundred bucks." She picked up the shattered remains of her cell phone and turned to the boy. "And I'm not a reporter, bird brain. I'm the editor of the student paper, and I can take pictures anywhere on this campus."

"Rosie, we'll talk tomorrow. Go home. Now," I interrupted before the boy could reply. I could see her hands trembling as she shoved the pieces of phone into her jacket pocket. She gave me a sour look and walked off without a word to the others or me.

After Rosie had disappeared into the darkness, I turned to the two remaining on the lawn. "She is the editor," I said. "And she does have the right to photograph what's going on."

"This is private property," said the boy.

"The house may be. But this area outside is Mountain West University property," I replied. "And you owe Rosie Jenkins a new cell phone."

The tall girl shook her head and spit on the lawn.

"Not very ladylike," said a tall older woman coming toward me from the direction of the construction. "Good evening, Dean Solaris."

I recognized her from her television appearances. Danica Boerum, a woman I believed to be an out-and-out racist. I stared at her. How did she know my name?

A ghost of a smile played on her face. She was not conventionally pretty, yet she was remarkably good-looking. Wide-set brown eyes, straight nose, firm chin, and thick, dazzling white hair she wore close-cropped so it haloed her faced. She extended her hand. "Danica Boerum. I saw you speak at a journalism conference in Cincinnati a year ago. You were eloquent about the protections of The First Amendment."

Oh, shit. Did I give her some tips on how to use the First Amendment to defend her own awful opinions?

Her hand remained outstretched, and I took it briefly. It felt like ice. Or perhaps it was my own hand that was chilled to the bone. "Ms. Boerum," I mumbled. "I gather you're going to visit here in the near future."

"I am," she said, gathering a thick white shawl around her shoulders. "Tonight I'm checking out the platform details. Hope to see you at my talk. Perhaps we can meet afterward and chat about freedom of speech." She turned back to the two men still in shadow by the house.

Chat? Not unless you put a gun to my head. "I hope you'll allow photographers," I called to her retreating back.

"Just official ones. No amateurs." She waved her hand.

"So that's the dreaded Danica Boerum," I said out loud once in my car. And I shook her hand. What an idiot. I reached into the glove compartment and pulled out a sani-wipe and scrubbed my hand vigorously. That's what you get for being stupidly appropriate.

Granted, Boerum had been polite and pleasant. There had been no trace of animus or hostility, although she must have known I despised everything she stood for, even if nothing she said to me had touched upon her racist speeches, her insistent calling for "a purer America." I hated everything I'd ever heard about her, especially her drumbeat argument that the Founding Fathers had intended America to be a nation founded solely for the descendants of Europeans, a nation that should be governed exclusively by men who looked as white as the signers of the Declaration.

I had been following her in the media for several months, thinking the stories on her would be a good case for my journalism students to study. Her speeches had caused at least two violent campus riots. Six students and two faculty members had been seriously injured at her last appearance. She was persona non grata at most of the nation's universities. In spite of her extremist views, she drew audiences of a thousand or more. Almost every one of her events had ended in rioting, gunshot wounds, split lips, cops with face shields, and students in handcuffs. I remembered the television coverage and the grisly picture on Facebook of a girl with her front teeth broken. I swallowed hard. Now the trouble Danica Boerum caused was coming to my campus.

What was it Justice Holmes had said about the importance of free thought? "Not just for those that agree with us but freedom for the thought that we hate."

Freedom for the thought that we hate. Was I prepared to agree with Holmes? I was a First Amendment fanatic, according to several friends. And the freedom to utter even hateful words was the root of my own deep belief in free speech. I knew I would have to keep telling myself that over and over again when Boerum came to Mountain West University.

The next morning, I decided *freedom for the thought that we hate* was a tough concept to digest before breakfast.

Footfall on the stairs intruded on my thoughts. Detective Joe Morgan had been living in my house for six months, but the sound of his rapid descent from the bedroom we shared still startled me before I had finished my coffee.

"You're later than usual," I said.

"Court this morning. Judge wants us there at ten. I thought I would take it easy until then." He treated me to a grin that always seemed unexpected in his rugged chief of detectives face. He leaned down, pulled back my hair and kissed the side of my neck. I could smell his shaving cream and the touch of his fingers in my hair produced predictable warmth. He walked to the stove still dressed only in his shorts. His shoulders were wide and his back was long and muscular. He had played basketball in college and his legs still looked eligible. A replica of the statue of David in my kitchen. Lucky me.

He turned to give me an amused look with his dark green eyes. His face opened again into a crooked smile as he reached one long, well-defined arm for the cast-iron skillet hanging by the stove. "Can I make you an omelet?"

"I wish you could. But I have a deans' meeting in an hour and there's always way too much food there. And, of course, I always eat it."

Pity. Joe's omelets were worth making anyone late for work.

He broke eggs into a bowl and stirred vigorously. "All carbs at a university deans' meeting, my love. I'm offering protein here. Fresh eggs, shallots, cheddar cheese. Plus, fresh orange juice and a little morning sex. Keep you slim and satisfied."

"Stop. Stop. I'm already late." I sighed loudly enough for him to hear, stood up, gently passed my fingertips over his impressive shoulders and headed for the stairs.

"Your loss," he said to a shallot and sliced it.

The drive to the university took me along a two-lane road that cut through the west side of Landry, Nevada. Spring had come early after an unusually mild winter and, much as I worry about global warming, I had to say that the exceptionally high temperatures benefitted the beauty of northern Nevada. It was still March and, instead of snow, the daffodils were massed and brilliant on the front lawns of my neighbors' homes. Puffy white pear trees and pink flowering plums lined the street. The air was warm and the sky bright blue. If I'd owned a convertible, I would have put the top down and let the wind ruin my carefully combed hair.

I turned onto the main drag in Landry and slowed to

admire the elegant white brick theater that housed our opera and ballet companies. For a small city, ours was blessed with the active cultural life characteristic of a university town.

Landry was located about an hour from Reno and was a four-hour drive from San Francisco. Mountain West University was Landry's largest employer and the city had grown up around the campus. Luckily, we were still a community of low one- and two-story buildings, so you could see the Sierra Nevada from almost everywhere you went. The mountaintops at thirteen thousand feet above sea level were still covered with snow that often lasted until July.

It was the beginning of my favorite time of year and my mood was light in spite of my concerns about Danica Boerum's appearance. I tried to push my worries aside and concentrate on the beauty of the main entrance to the university and enjoy the drive through the clear morning. I thought about Joe. After almost two years of a back-and-forth love affair, he had finally decided to move into my house last fall. For two months afterwards, he kept his old apartment, which made me nervous, but finally, at Christmas—perhaps as a gift to me—he abandoned his ambivalence and the last of his books and records found their places on the shelves in my living room.

Sadie Hawkins was right. One afternoon during a long walk she had said, "Red, you are deliriously in love and it is most becoming. I have never seen you look so radiant."

Sadie was my best friend, in spite of our age difference. I was thirty-seven and she had just turned seventy. I was a newly appointed university dean and she was the retired Dean of Liberal Arts, wiser and more experienced than I and as close to me as a surrogate mother.

Her delight in my new circumstances warmed me. Sadie had been opposed to my candidacy for the dean's job, but now seemed rather pleased that I had won it after a long and controversial search. She was even more pleased that Detective Joe Morgan and I were finally living together and, better yet, not quarreling.

"Maybe if you stick to education and let Joe do all the criminal investigations, your relationship will be less turbulent," Sadie had said at our weekly lunch.

"Maybe, but I'm really good at figuring out details," I said. "He may get angry about how I do it, but Joe acknowledges I have been helpful with his cases. I'm good at strategic thinking. I read clues well. I make connections. Joe says he admires that."

"I'm sure you are very useful in tracking down bad guys. But you drive Joe crazy when you risk your own safety."

She was right. Joe hated it when I took it into my head to go out on my own to solve a puzzle or a crime, worse yet to participate in the hunt and capture. Twice, I had come close to being killed. But how do you achieve success without taking risks?

And success was something I thoroughly enjoyed. I pulled up in the parking lot of the Mountain West School of Journalism at a space marked "Reserved for the Dean of Journalism." I never thought I would so enjoy parking my car in the morning. With my new dean's salary, I had treated myself to a hybrid Toyota that suited my liberal sensibilities and still gleamed in the sunlight.

I smiled again when I saw "Dean of Journalism: Dr. Meredith Solaris—Room 300" at the top of the directory in the school lobby. I had fought hard for the privilege of running my school and won out over some serious opposition. The memory of that triumph always cheered me up.

"I don't know what in the hell you've got to look so sunny about." The voice belonged to Phyllis Baker, Professor of Media Graphics and a good friend. Tall and dark, she appeared especially severe standing by the elevator, clutching her briefcase and frowning as I approached. Her lovely face looked grim and her voice sounded choked.

"Just enjoying the morning," I replied. "What's got you down?"

"Did you see the paper? Danica Boerum is coming here to spread us with her filthy philosophy."

The elevator doors opened and I pushed the button for the third floor. Phyllis folded her arms tightly cross her chest and leaned against the elevator wall, a study in disapproval. "If Danica Boerum had her way, I'd be deported even though I've been an American citizen for a dozen years."

"Calm down, my dear Dr. Baker. Legitimate and law-abiding citizens like you can't be deported. It's unlikely Danica Boerum will ever get her way. She represents a very small minority of bigots."

"Not small enough for me. I wish the administration would ban her speech here."

"Nonsense. We're journalists. We don't ban speech. We defend it."

I got an angry grunt for that. The doors opened and Phyllis headed out. I grasped her arm. "I'm sure everything will be all right, Phil. Most of the faculty and students will boycott Boerum's appearance and, a week later, she'll be completely forgotten."

Phyllis turned toward me, her black eyes flooded. "Unless there's violence, Red. Unless there's violence." Phyllis had escaped the genocide of non-Arab Sudanese in Darfur. She and her parents arrived in America with nothing but their clothes and a powerful work ethic that had put Phyllis through college. Now a grown woman with a family of her own and a distinguished career, any reminders of her childhood filled her with old terror.

I hugged her shoulders. She pulled away, her eyes narrow

and her mouth a straight, bitter line. She pulled off her jacket and flung it over her shoulders, narrowly missing my head. "We both know how racism damages a place and how awful things happen when people get riled up."

No comforting reassurances came to mind and I stood silent, looking up at the tears in my friend's eyes. Then I tried again: "Freedom for the thought that we hate, Phil. You remember that."

"I'll tell you what I remember about hate. It has an ugly face covered in sweat, eyes bulging out and full of rage, teeth bared back to the gum line. Black or white, it's the face of the primitive, ready to kill you just because you're different. It's a face you never want to see on this campus."

Phyllis turned on her heel and headed down the hall. She moved swiftly, her bare ebony arms pumping, her hips swinging as if to emphasize her fury. As I watched her, I thought again how little I understood what my friend had endured. My own childhood had been lonely and difficult, but Dr. Phyllis Baker had gone through hell and seen sights no child should ever have witnessed.

Maybe she was right. What did I know about racism? Cruel, violent racism, not just words hurled across a police line, but a gang of men on camels and horses with swords in their hands and death in their eyes.

What did I even know about discrimination? I'd been hurt but never excluded, bullied but never denied access. In Phyllis Baker's mind, was I just some bleeding heart Caucasian defending free speech because I had no idea how much pain some speech could cause?

My head started to ache. *Enough. Go to work.* I turned toward my office at the other end of the hall.

Chapter 2

The early morning's good mood did not return, even with the sight of dappled sunlight and tall trees visible through the large windows of my office. The campus of Mountain West is one of the loveliest in America. Wide green lawns, flowering trees in spring and masses of bright annuals all summer and fall. When the thick snow falls in winter, the elegant brick buildings and the frosted trees take on the look of a New England Christmas card. I never ceased congratulating myself on applying for work at this institution.

My large glass desk in front of the windows was a model of neatness. No thanks to me. That was entirely to Nell's credit. I had the best dean's assistant on the campus and was grateful every day.

The agenda for the deans' meeting was centered on the blotter flanked by a slim file of letters I was supposed to sign before the day was over. Two upholstered armchairs, a couch and a large glass coffee table completed the room. My mother's china tea service centered the table. We never used the delicate cups because everyone wanted strong coffee in mugs, but the tea service looked welcoming and it was the only one of my late mother's possessions I'd ever wanted.

When I was officially named Dean of Journalism and moved into the two-room suite, I'd been happy to abandon the former dean's conference table in favor of my own office décor. I wanted people to feel comfortable, not confronted, when they sat opposite me.

I'd also been happy to order a new desk for Nell's office next to mine. And we had immediately agreed to put a computer and a coffee pot in the sitting area outside so students could check schedules and work while waiting to see me. My assistant has an unfailing habit of making the well-being of our students her top priority.

"You have five minutes to drink this and then you need to get going," said Nell, coming through the door with a steaming cup in her hand. "They've moved the deans' meeting to the administration building across campus."

Nell's gray curls nestled around her face. If Sadie thought I was radiant in love, she should have seen my assistant. A widow in her early sixties, Nell still looked remarkably girlish.

"How go the wedding plans?" I asked. Nell was about to marry Wynan Congers, a tall retired police chief with a face so handsome it could have taken him to Hollywood instead of into law enforcement.

"They're going well. We're keeping it small. Just family and a few friends." She smiled. "You and Joe, of course."

"We're looking forward to it."

"And Sadie."

"I'm glad you're asking Sadie. She spends too much time alone these days. Is Wynan inviting any single friends of his?"

"Maybe one." Nell's smile became mysterious. Clearly she was keeping a secret and enjoying it thoroughly. She'd better not be planning to introduce Sadie to some old retired cop. Except for Joe, law enforcement types were not Sadie's preferred companions.

"Red, you'd better get going. The meeting starts at nine sharp."

*   *   *

Back outdoors again into the inviting high desert warmth. The whole campus seemed to be in preparation for the new season. The path to the administration building took me past rose bushes just starting to leaf out and a line of purple hyacinths in front of white narcissus. The Mountain West colors. My mood lit up again. The joy of Nell's impending marriage had overcome my concerns about Phyllis's fears and the Purist event to come. I climbed the wide steps to the administration building just as the carillon in the clock tower chimed the hour. I would get to the meeting on time.

The deans of Mountain West University gathered every second Tuesday of the month to engage in discussions led by our Provost, Manny Lorenzo. The administration conference room was large and comfortably furnished with upholstered leather chairs. It was also abuzz with conversation about Danica Boerum's impending visit. The cinnamon buns and Danish pastry on their usual silver trays lay undisturbed. No one was eating or sitting down. Everyone was milling about.

"When the provost gets here I plan to ask him to insist The Purists cancel her. No student group should be allowed to bring a woman like that to a university. And no campus should tolerate hate speech." Bridget Thomas, Dean of The College of Economics, was holding forth. Loud and opinionated barely described her.

"Now, Bridget, she doesn't actually say she hates anyone, including our minorities. She just acts as if they were not part of the deal and talks about America's proud white European heritage and the 1776 crowd," said Bill Verden, the Dean of Science. A man I liked better than most, humorous and reasonable.

"But her message is clear," said the Dean of Engineering.

"There's really no mistaking the intent. She wants everyone who looks like me to leave this country and go back to some original home country. I've visited my grandparents in Korea, but I have no desire to live there. Danica Boerum doesn't recognize me as a native-born American, and that's infuriating."

"I understand," said Bill, putting his hand on his colleague's shoulder. "But doesn't Boerum have the right to speak even if her opinion is despicable? What about freedom of speech and the First Amendment?"

Bridget turned to me. "You're our resident First Amendment advocate. What do you think?" Down went my mood again.

"I think we are a university and should encourage the free exchange of opinion whenever possible," I said, dodging the real thrust of Bridget's question and her clear intent to involve me in a lengthy argument.

"And that's just the point," said Provost Manny Lorenzo, propelling his sturdy frame into the room through a door that connected to his office. "So don't bother to ask, because I don't have any intention of banning Danica Boerum's speech to a campus group and neither does President Stoddard." Manny eased his big body into a chair at the head of the table and flashed a wide grin to remind us all how much we liked him.

"Even if she starts a riot like she did at..."

"I plan to have heavy security," said Manny. "And I will meet with all the student leaders and pass the word that all who go should expect to behave like civilized men and women. No shouting her down. No rioting. Remain polite even if you don't like what you hear. You don't have to go."

"Are you going?"

Manny's eyes sparkled. "Of course I'm going. I always take the opportunity to listen to views that oppose mine. Keeps me sharp. Besides, if trouble starts, I'll add myself to the security force. I can be terrifying when necessary." A nervous laugh followed. Manny was not just big and beefy, he worked out. "Remember, I'm the Chicano kid, raised on the mean streets and always ready to prove how tough I am." He busied himself with papers in front of him. "Now, let's get to work."

We slowly took our seats.

Back in my office two hours later, I stared at the pile of documents that had been handed out at the deans' meeting: budget summaries, recommendations for promotion and tenure, proposed changes in Mountain West degree requirements. All the stuff of academic administration that took time away from the joy of teaching my one course in Media Ethics and meeting with my students.

Fate brought me a distraction.

"Rosie's here," said Nell, standing in my doorway.

Rosie Jenkins was not quite five feet two inches tall, skin as pale as milk, freckled nose and cheeks under blue eyes that always seemed to penetrate into your head and read your mind when she talked to you. I had known her since her first day as a freshman. She was introduced to me by an old friend, Sonia Ortiz. Sonia was a psychologist who worked with girls who'd been rescued from sex-trafficking rings.

Rosie was one of the rare escapees who'd been rescued from the sex trade at fourteen and then worked her way through high school and into our university. As part of her therapy, she'd written about her troubled childhood, her time as a child prostitute on the streets of Los Angeles and her recovery, thanks to therapy and the help of a compassionate cop who had arrested her and then persuaded her to go to a rehab facility in another state.

Rosie had published her story in the student paper, which

started her off in journalism. When it came to good writing, all she got was better and better. I liked almost all my students, but I truly loved Rosie, bright and brave with the fighting spirit of a challenged terrier.

"How's it goin', Red?" she said, plopping into the chair in front of my desk. Journalism students call those of us who teach them by our first names. We like it that way.

"It goes well, thank you. I gather you have recovered from your encounter with the Purists last night."

The merry look vanished. "I probably should thank you for coming to my rescue, but I might have enjoyed mixing it up with them, especially that tall broad. I could have taken her in the first round."

"Then again, you might not have enjoyed getting hurt."

Rosie shifted in her chair. "Yeah, I know. But those people are real pussies, Red. They're all talk and no muscle. I'm stronger than you think. I know something about street fighting."

"I'm still glad your street knowledge did not have to be put to use. So, are you still planning to do a piece on the Danica Boerum speech at the Purist house? Or did last night's adventure curb your appetite?"

"Not at all. I'm planning on a story next week even if I have to use a stock photo, dammit."

"That's my girl."

"Maybe I'll preview it in the podcast tonight. It will be a better story if I can get a good quote from the always fair-minded Dean of Journalism..." Rosie's freckles danced with amusement.

"Oh God, Rosie. Could you let me pass on this one? It's what the students think that really matters, and the last thing I want to do is stir up more hard feelings."

"Faculty opinion matters too. I'm afraid you have to say

something, because all the other professors I've called this morning either ducked me or ranted on about what a disgrace it was to invite Boerum and how violence was a guaranteed outcome."

I decided against mentioning my own encounter with Boerum. I was still ashamed about the handshake. But Rosie was right. I couldn't very well defend the right of free speech if I refused to speak myself. Rosie pulled a notebook out of her backpack and began to write.

"Okay, I guess I should step up, like it or not. How about this: The Purists are a legitimate student organization and have been for several years. As such, they can invite any speaker they want. This is an open campus where freedom of expression is encouraged, even if we don't agree with a particular point of view. How's that?" The words sounded evenhanded even if the sentiment stuck in my throat. I didn't tell her about Manny's security plans. That was his business.

"You don't think she'll cause trouble?"

"Oh, I don't know. Boerum is all about trouble. But I do know that an American campus should be able to withstand the expression of unpopular opinion without starting a riot. Tell your readers to stay away if they don't approve of what she has to say. The last thing we need around here is a protest that starts a fight."

"No dice, Red. Seems to me I recall you teaching us in ethics class to value the opinion of those who oppose us. To seek out those with whom we disagree and listen to their ideas even if we are not persuaded. You said it would improve the quality of our thinking."

"I did, and it does. But, at the same time, I want to be sensitive to those faculty and students who would find it very hard to listen to Boerum's brand of undiluted bigotry."

"Would you call her views hate speech?"

"If you listen to her, she doesn't say she hates anyone or that we should hate anyone. She doesn't use derogatory terms or epithets. She outlines her theory that the best government is an all-white government. She believes our minority citizens are—how does she put it?—'talented and industrious, but not ready for leadership positions.' She's careful and keeps her voice well-modulated. Unlike most dogmatists, she never shouts."

"She ignores the fact that a majority of children entering kindergarten this year are non-white. Someday soon minority is going to mean white people."

"And that's what makes her speeches so appealing to those who are afraid of the very change you describe."

"Well, okay. But I think she's a fanatic and her speech is just hate speech in a soft voice, which doesn't make it less virulent. I spent a lot of time on the internet doing research on her talks as well as staring at pictures of her this morning."

"I've studied her too."

A shadow passed over Rosie's face. "Danica Boerum reminds me of someone. There was a girl I knew back in LA when I was in the life. She was a bottom bitch in another gang and she had the same hard eyes as Boerum does in her photographs."

"A bottom bitch?"

The shadow deepened. "A bottom bitch is an older girl who manages all the younger ones in the gang. Keeps them in line, almost a substitute for the pimp when he's away. Some I knew were as mean as rattlesnakes."

Whenever Rosie told me something about her previous life, it made my blood pressure mount thinking about what she must have gone through from the age of twelve until she was rescued at fourteen.

"Chances are Boerum lives far away from anything as disreputable as the sex trade. Purity is, after all, her mantra."

Rosie closed her notebook and, for a minute, her eyes. "Did I tell you I saw my cousin at the mall in Reno last week?"

"No. The younger cousin who lived with you in LA?"

Rosie nodded. "Cathy. I think I told you she had run away from my mom's house last year. No big surprise there. The prince of darkness who married my mother probably made a move on her after I left."

"Oh, Rosie. What happened to you just sickens me."

"Me too. But now I'm worried about Cathy. In spite of all my warnings about men who say they'll help, I now discover she's being trafficked by a pimp who renamed her Snowbird. She's only thirteen. Her hair's dyed silver blonde and she wears about a half-gallon of makeup."

"Did you get a chance to talk to her?"

"For a little while. Mostly she talked about this guy she met at a bus station and what he'd promised her. But just as I was going to try to set her straight, persuade her to come with me, her pimp—a really nasty mother—showed up and dragged her away." Rosie drew a deep breath. She had once told me her cousin Cathy was the only member of her family she loved. She still felt guilty about leaving Cathy behind to suffer abuse from a deeply depressed mother and a predatory stepfather. Her plan was to find an apartment for herself and Cathy after she graduated and found a job to support both of them. Sounded like that plan was in jeopardy.

Rosie put her notebook into her backpack and walked over to one of the tall windows. Her shoulders shook under her thick sweater and for a moment, I thought she was crying. Still facing the window, she said, "Red, I need a favor."

"You know I'll do whatever I can. How can I help?"

"After I saw Cathy at the mall, I went to the Reno police to see if they had anyone who specialized in rescuing underage kids from sex trafficking. They do have a special squad, but yesterday they told me no one on the squad was able to find her or anyone who knows anything about a girl called Snowbird." Rosie turned from the window. "So the other reason I'm here this morning is I was wondering if your Detective Morgan could..."

"I'll talk to Joe tonight."

Rosie walked to my desk and stretched her small hand to mine. "Thank you so much. You're the best." She reached into her backpack and produced a small color photo, obviously a school picture. "This is what Cathy looked like when she was eleven, before she ran away." The photo showed a dark-haired girl with the same freckles and milky skin she shared with Rosie.

"She looks like you. She could be your little sister."

"I loved her as my little sister. That's why I have to get her out."

Chapter 3

Joe had a particular empathy for criminalized children, and I knew he would help Rosie if he could. He was different from a number of the law enforcement people I had met in Ohio when I worked for the newspaper. For that matter, he was different from many in Nevada. It made him angry when members of his profession described prostitution as a petty crime. Or a victimless crime. It made me angry that most of the good citizens I knew thought all prostitution in Nevada was legal and wondered what the fuss was about. The true fact: prostitution is legal in Nevada only in counties of fewer than four hundred thousand and only in legal brothels. That eliminated my county, as well as Washoe County, where Reno is located.

From what Rosie had told me and from my own research, I knew the average age was twelve to fourteen for girls entering the sex trade. Most were runaways and throwaways. More than 70 percent of them had been sexually abused and certainly neglected and unprotected at home.

Once a child had run away or been thrown out, she could be approached by a trafficker within forty-eight hours of leaving home because they could spot her easily—a girl with low self-esteem who just wanted a loving relationship she couldn't find at home.

*   *   *

Joe was in the kitchen preparing our dinner. The photo of Rosie's cousin Cathy was still in my pocket. I'd kept looking at the child's pale delicate features all through the afternoon and never put it in my briefcase. I pulled it out one more time.

"Shrimp marinara tonight. What's that?" said Joe, glancing up from his skillet. The smell of browning butter filled the air. I showed him the photo. "Hmm. Looks a lot like Rosie Jenkins," he said, stirring the golden froth then spooning in some diced onion. Since he moved in with his special skillets and sharp knives, Joe did all the cooking in my house. It was his particular pleasure to make what all who knew him considered the best fish and pasta dishes in the state. I considered myself blessed.

Charlie, my Golden Retriever, groaned and lifted up from his dog bed as if it was an incredible effort to greet me. His golden eyes fixed me with a bored stare, but then he made it over for a scratch behind the ears. After all, I was still the one who fed him even if his heart belonged to the alpha male now scraping the skillet and adding tomatoes.

"Rosie gave me this picture of her cousin, Cathy. She encountered her with her pimp last week in Reno. Cathy's the one she told us about who ran away from the same home that drove Rosie into the streets of Los Angeles."

"And probably the same mother's disgusting husband. I'll bet that bastard still hasn't done time for raping kids. I wouldn't mind getting my hands on that son of a bitch." Joe's contempt was visible in his face.

"If only you could have, or some cop in LA could have. Remember how she told us that after she fought him off, her stepfather dragged her out of her mother's house and threw her in the back of his car? He drove downtown and sold Rosie to a trafficker for a hundred and fifty dollars."

Joe turned back to concentrate on the sauce in his frying pan, but I could see his shoulders tighten with anger. "I remember Rosie telling us the trafficker was kind to her at first so she didn't run away. He promised to get her an apartment and a job in a supermarket. Not that she had any reason to go back home."

"And if it hadn't been for a good cop in LA, Rosie might still be with him and still be 'in the life,' as she calls it."

"Or still on the internet. That's where most of the sex-for-money deals are made now." Joe lowered the heat under his sauce and poured us each a glass of wine. His face was flushed. "It makes me want to throw up. A guy comes to Vegas or Reno for business, or an event like a rodeo or a show. He has a good time, a few drinks, then goes up to his hotel room, brings up a site on his laptop and orders a girl brought to his room. If he likes them young, he orders a kid."

"Is it always visitors?"

"Christ, no. Sometimes it's a Nevada resident who just likes sex with underage girls." Joe's face grew redder with his anger. "And the public tolerates this because they think all the young girls are over eighteen or prostitutes imported from poor countries."

"Haven't some of those girls been kidnapped?"

"Some. But a lot of the young girls being trafficked in the west are runaways from Nevada and California. A Reno cop I know told me 50 percent of the girls are from this area. This is a transportation hub as well as a major tourist area. The girls were more likely lured away, or found as runaways, but not abducted. Rosie was dragged away from home and sold, but she stayed with her pimp. Many of these children stay with their pimps even when they might escape."

"It amazes me how few people care about this crime."

Joe swallowed a large mouthful of wine. Both of us had

talked about this before. We knew sex trafficking was the second-largest growing crime in the country. In many places, it had replaced drug trafficking. Unlike cocaine or heroin, sex was a renewable commodity. A pimp could sell the same girl over and over again. And the sentences were much lighter if he got caught.

Joe's anger transferred to me. I could feel my blood heat up. I drained half the wineglass. "You know, if some man we knew as a neighbor or a colleague at work went to a hotel and had sex with a twelve-year-old, we'd label him a pedophile and have him arrested."

Joe's groan was deep and fierce. He walked to the kitchen window. "I guess ordering online and paying the kid who shows up gives a man who thinks of himself as respectable permission to do the unthinkable."

For a minute or so the only sound in the room was the light bubbling of tomato sauce.

"Rosie says the Reno PD hasn't found her cousin yet and wonders if you could help."

Joe turned back from the window. "Reno PD has some good men and women specializing in sex trafficking. If they haven't been able to find the girl, it's possible her pimp moved her to another city. Maybe the encounter with Rosie scared him off."

I walked over to Joe and put my hand on his arm as he stirred the sauce. "Would you mind looking into it?"

Joe kissed my forehead.

I knew he'd do what I asked. He never turned me down.

After dinner, I called Rosie, and she showed up with her cheeks flushed pink as if she'd run all the way from her apartment to my house. Her words were rushed. "Thanks so much, Detective Morgan. This really means a lot to me."

Joe settled Rosie on the living room couch and took the chair opposite her. He leaned forward, notebook in hand, green eyes focused, voice professionally gentle. I loved the way Joe responded to people who needed help.

"Rosie, I'm not sure how much I'll be able to do, but I will call the chief in Reno first thing tomorrow and find out what they ran into."

"Thank you."

"Don't thank me yet. The Reno cops are very thorough and experienced, so it's quite likely your cousin has just been transferred to another location. There's major trafficking in several western cities, especially those that draw a tourist crowd."

Rosie's shoulders slumped. "I know. The creep who pimped me out took me to Dallas and Vegas. Fortunately, he always brought me back to LA, where I was rescued." She looked intently from Joe to me and back to Joe. Her small frame twitched. "What I hope for Cathy is a good cop like the one who found me and took me away to a rehab center in Colorado." A small smile accompanied a tilt of her head. "I'm told you're a good cop, Detective Morgan."

Joe returned the smile. "You don't have to flatter me, Rosie. I'm going to do what I can tomorrow. Now, tell me what I need to know about your cousin."

"Want some coffee to go with this?" I asked.

Joe nodded and Rosie looked up at me. "Thanks, Red. That would be great." As I left for the kitchen I observed that their heads were close together, totally absorbed in Rosie's account.

Rosie described Cathy as about five foot three, thin frame, pale skin, small breasts, and short spiky very light blond hair. When Rosie had last seen her in the mall, Cathy wore thick black eyeliner under and over her blue eyes, plus silver shadow and thick mascara. She was dressed in a tight t-shirt and shorts, a denim jacket and high-top sneakers. "The point is to make sure she looked like a kid, but a sexy, available kid."

Joe's notes were detailed. Rosie's memory for the ways of teen trafficking victims was sharp and educated. "The idea is to get the john to think that she's a dumb kid who really likes sex and who really wants him bad. She'd almost do it for free, he's so attractive and she's so hot for him. Of course, she knows the pimp is watching her from a few feet away and she's scared to death of failing to make the deal. At the same time, she's sick to her stomach because the john is a bald, overweight forty-year-old."

"Can you describe Cathy's pimp?"

"Husky, round-faced, white, maybe Hispanic. Dark brown hair. Average height. I didn't talk to him long, but I suspect he came on to her as a huggy bear, recruited her with affection and then turned her out."

Joe had interrupted Rosie at that point. "Tell me about Cathy as a child."

Cathy had come to live with Rosie's mother and Rosie when she was three. Her parents were gone, a mother who had died of an overdose and a father, Rosie's uncle, who had been sentenced to twenty years for dealing. It was the imprisoned father who had requested his sister become Cathy's guardian.

Rosie was seven when Cathy arrived and the two had become sisters almost immediately. Cathy was charming and bubbly, loved games, dolls and ice cream.

"What flavor?" asked Joe, without looking up from his notes.

Rosie thought for a moment. "Strawberry with sprinkles. Does it matter?"

"Everything matters."

*   *   *

An hour and a half later, Rosie said goodnight and Joe put his notebook back in his jacket pocket.

"Do you think you can help her?"

Joe leaned his tall body against the frame of the kitchen door, his hand going up, fingers idly playing along the top of the doorframe. "Hard to say. But I think, instead of calling Reno PD, I'm going to drive to Reno tomorrow and sit down with some of their task force people. See what they know and don't know."

As I said before, Joe never turned me down. Never let me down either. His particular soft spot for children was made more intense by his memory of a dead boy in Chicago years ago. The boy had been dressed in a puffy coat and a ski mask to make him look older while he tried to rob a delicatessen. The gun he had aimed at Joe was defective, but Joe hadn't known that and fired.

Long after he had left Chicago PD and moved back to Landry, Joe had still not forgiven himself. So whenever a crime involved a child, Joe Morgan made sure he was in on the investigation. Day and night if necessary.

Chapter 4

The next morning, five minutes after I entered my office, I received a surprise visit from the provost. I learned some time ago that the slender chairs in front of my desk were no good for men as sizeable as Manny Lorenzo, so I steered him to one of my large upholstered armchairs and sat facing him on the couch. Nell brought us coffee, placed the mugs quietly on the coffee table and then left, closing the door behind her.

Manny stirred milk and too much sugar into his coffee. His massive chest rose as he took a deep breath. "Danica Boerum," he said. "I know what I think. What do you think?"

"I think you need to talk it through."

"Because..."

"Because you walked clear across campus to get to my office when all you had to do was pick up the phone."

"I miss being in a journalism school." He winked. "Everything is always so black and white."

"We're in color now. Even shades of gray."

Manny put down his mug and laced his fingers behind his head. Still youthful-looking, the lines in his tan face had deepened and gray streaks had shown up in his thick dark hair since he took on the management of all the academic matters at Mountain West. A dean's job is tough enough, a provost's even more demanding. I was flattered that Manny considered me his friend when he had a problem to work out. "Oh, Red, I despise everything that Danica Boerum stands for, but I cannot, absolutely cannot, bring myself to ban her from this campus."

"I despise her ideas too, but I think you're right."

Manny's features sagged with despair. His usually bright brown eyes looked confused and sad. "My parents would have given me hell if they knew what I felt bound to do here. My mother and father lived with anti-Mexican prejudice all their lives even though they came to America legally, became citizens, owned a business and put three kids through college."

"That must have been very hard for you to deal with."

"It was. My father was so resentful of what he had to endure, he told me that when he died, I was to take his body back to Guadalajara so he could be buried in friendly soil. My mother asked the same thing." He rubbed his hands together. "And now here's their well-heeled, well-educated son about to let a bigot speak on this very campus."

My heart ached for my good friend. I tried to think of some way to comfort him. "Maybe the way to think about it is to accept that Boerum was invited by a student organization for a theoretically private event. She's not speaking at an official university event. She's not even appearing in one of our classrooms. She's not coming as a commencement speaker to address an entire graduating class and their families." I paused. "I mean, we're not in the same position as those schools who felt they had to disinvite Condoleezza Rice and Christine Lagarde from their commencement speeches just because some students and university staff didn't like their policies."

"I hated that," said Manny.

"So did I. I was embarrassed for them."

"Rice and Lagarde weren't racists or even radicals. They were just distinguished women with different opinions. But I agree with you. I couldn't understand why the students at those universities couldn't bear to listen to someone with whom they disagreed for twenty minutes. There was always the slim chance they could have learned something." Manny's face had relaxed a bit as he reminded himself that he was probably making a reasonable decision.

"Students are increasingly touchy these days. I have a complaint on my desk about one of my professors showing photographs of soldiers discovering the piles of dead bodies in Auschwitz," I said.

"Good Lord, why?"

"Some of the more sensitive think they should have been excused from class before the photos were shown so their sensibilities could have been spared."

Manny rolled his eyes. "And these students want to go into journalism?"

"Yep. I have a few who think today's journalism is all just Comedy Central and *Entertainment Tonight*."

"Oh, I remember those. The same ones who don't understand why they have to take geography—or, for God's sake, American History—when all they plan to do is cover plane crashes and human interest stories."

"I know. I'm not very sympathetic to them. If they want to work for any important media outlet, they'll have to be able to report on some dreadful events. That means having to cope with terrifying sights and sounds without losing their equilibrium."

"Psychologists and nurses have to be prepared for the same world. And all of them have to be prepared to work in a difficult world. Yet I have faculty in my office every day trying to educate their students on how to deal with trauma, and at the same time trying to figure out how to avoid discussions that trigger memories of negative experiences."

We both paused and reached again for our coffee mugs,

eager to avoid the direction we both knew our conversation would take.

"Any chance you could get the student Purists to hold their Danica Boerum event off campus?"

Manny frowned. "They bought that old fraternity house on campus so they could have a place to live and hold meetings. To feel safe, as they told me. They know they're unpopular. They plan to hold a private dinner inside followed by a speech under a big tent covering their front lawn and parking lot. They believe they have a right to have this meeting on campus."

"And what does Provost Lorenzo believe?"

"I grew up in journalism just like you. But even if I hadn't, I believe in the Constitution and in their First Amendment rights."

"But you're worried about violence."

"Yes. Not so much from Boerum or her staff, but from the audience. The same limited thinking that produced your student complaint often characterizes those people who will think it's all right to raise hell when you hate what someone else believes."

"Yet even with that worry, you're not going to ban Danica Boerum's appearance?" I said.

"Nope. Much as I'd like to, I'm not. Neither will President Stoddard. He won't attend her speech, but agrees with me that Boerum has a right to her dreadful opinions and the Purists have a right to listen to it."

"So, if you've already decided it's okay to let her speak, what did you need to see me for?"

Manny took a final swig of coffee, rose from his chair and headed for the door. "I was hoping you could somehow talk me out of it."

"Sorry, pal."

*   *   *

After Manny left, Nell came in to pick up the coffee mugs. "Provost looked unhappy."

"He's worried, and he should be." A wave of nausea hit me. Maybe I was under more tension than I realized, or heading toward a bout of flu. I steadied myself on the edge of my desk.

"You okay?"

"Do I have any appointments this morning? I think I may go home for the rest of the day. I seem to be coming down with something."

"A student wants to file a grade appeal and said he needed your advice and Rosie Jenkins called. Wanted to see you this afternoon after her last class."

"Tell the student to speak to Edwin Cartwell about the grade appeal. Edwin gives good advice. Unless, of course, the appeal is against one of his grades, in which case, you talk to the student. You know more about academic procedures than anyone around here."

Nell's chin went up a notch. "Thank you. What about Rosie?"

"Tell her to call me at home later this afternoon. Maybe I'll be up to a meeting by then."

The nausea stayed with me on the drive home. I called my doctor when I got into the house.

"Take a nap," she said. "Drink lots of liquids. I'll try to fit you in tomorrow if you're still feeling poorly."

The phone awoke me at four in the afternoon. It was Rosie.

"I think I saw Cathy again," she said. "Just a glimpse. She was in the backseat of a car that drove by me as I was heading back from Reno this afternoon."

"Are you sure?"

"Pretty sure. The car stopped for a red light and I saw her face."

"Did she see you?"

"No, but I think her pimp saw me."

"Why don't you come over for dinner tonight? Joe went to the Reno Police Department today and maybe he'll have some news when he gets home."

My nausea had abated and I felt well enough to get up, pet and feed Charlie and then start a salad for dinner. Joe came in at about five thirty with wine and enough lamb chops for six. I told him I had invited Rosie to join us. "How'd it go in Reno? Any more about her cousin, Cathy?"

"Not much," he said, laying the chops out on the butcher block to trim them. "One of their guys thought he had spotted a girl with white-blond hair who matched the description of Cathy, but she disappeared before he could confirm it was her. And none of them have heard about anyone named Snowbird." He sliced the fat off the chop with expert swiftness. "But the Reno Chief and I did have a discussion about something else I need to tell you about."

"A discussion?"

"Sort of." Joe stopped his work and went over to the sink to wash his hands. Then he came over and put his hands on my shoulders. I had a queasy feeling that had nothing to do with my earlier nausea. This was Joe's approach to telling me something I didn't want to hear.

"Sweetheart, the sex trafficking in Reno has become a huge problem. It's not just individual pimps, but gangs...actually organized rings of them. The more I heard, the more I wanted to help, so I volunteered to take on an undercover assignment. Maybe I will be able to penetrate one of the larger rings."

"You volunteered? But you're not on the Reno force."

Joe kissed me gently. This was his way of reassuring me about something I wasn't going to like.

"I'm someone whose face isn't known in Reno. And someone who's had extensive undercover experience."

I looked up into his dark green eyes. Every time I thought of Joe going into a dangerous situation my heart rate sped up so much I thought I was going to pass out. I really didn't like the sound of this.

"You told me you went undercover in Chicago."

He kissed my forehead. "Several times. The last time was only for six weeks. Just a short time to catch a drug dealer. And it worked, Red. We nailed the guy, and I came out of it without a scratch."

Six weeks? No deal.

Joe sat down at the kitchen table. "I know you don't like this, but I really do have the experience Reno could use right now, and going undercover might help me get Rosie's cousin out of there. Landry PD is okay with this. I hope you will be too."

I sat facing him. I loved Joe's face when he was trying to talk me into agreeing with him. His eyes got dark and warm and his lower lip jutted out in a particularly appealing way. He smiled. "Please tell me you don't have a problem with my going undercover in Reno, just for a week or two."

"You really want to do this, don't you?"

His head tilted to one side and his voice lowered to a whisper. "I do. I see it as a chance to help free some kids."

That did it. Rescuing even one child from the horror of the sex trade would mean an enormous amount to Joe. It might even be his way of seeking redemption for the boy in Chicago. There was no way I could object.

I put my hand on his and started to say something supportive when the doorbell rang. Rosie, clear-eyed and determined, stood on my doorstep.

*   *   *

For the first half hour, we chatted about everything except the true nature of Rosie's reason for being with us a second night in a row. Joe's lamb chops were broiled to perfection and he had chosen a smooth Pinot Noir to accompany them. But there was no avoiding talk about the sex trade. "You two are great, and smarter about this than most people, but even you enlightened beings really have no idea what it's like for the girls," said Rosie, idly pushing salad greens around her plate. "First of all, you've run away from home because it's impossible there, so when the life gets hard, you can't call your family, because they're even worse than your pimp."

"This may sound naïve, but do any of the girls ever call a women's shelter or the police?" I asked.

Rosie's eyes rolled up to the ceiling. "It's not naïve, but this is what's so hard to explain. When it begins, you're probably not looking to be rescued. The guy who found you in a bus station or on the street, or seduced you over the internet, has convinced you he really loves you and that he's the one who is rescuing you from an evil stepdad or Mom's boyfriend who comes into your room at night. The guy insists you're the only one for him and he's going to take you away from all the hell at home."

"Why are pimps so attractive? The few I've seen look pretty creepy to me."

"That's because you're a college dean and satin shirts and gold chains don't turn you on."

Joe added, "And you're not a desperate twelve-year-old."

Rosie pressed on, "Even after your pimp turns you out, he's still sympathetic and loving. He gets you clothes and food and makeup. He makes sure you have a place to stay. And if he's running other girls, friends to talk to."

"What are the other girls like?"

"A lot like me. It's a myth that all the girls in the sex trade have been brought here from Asia or Eastern Europe. Most of the ones in my group were Americans from California and Nevada. White, Black, Hispanic, usually runaways from troubled homes. Girls who hooked up with older men who promised them love, excitement and a glamorous life."

"Glamorous?"

Rosie's mouth formed a bitter grin. "Yeah, glamorous, believe it or not. We were told we'd have the kind of life that comes with pretty clothes and fancy hairstyles and dinners out and dancing at nightclubs. That was the usual line."

"And you fall for it."

"Of course, it's the first fulfilling relationship you've ever had. It just doesn't last long."

It was my turn to fiddle with my food instead of eating it. "So, after promising to love you forever, the pimp taught you how to use your looks and your youth and sexuality to make men give you money. Then he kept the money."

"You got it. He said he was keeping the money safe for your future, but you soon figured out he was keeping the money for his future. My pimp made six figures a year. As for taking care of you, that meant putting you up in shabby rental houses and cheap motels and feeding you meals from fast food joints."

"And beating you?" I could hardly believe that the bright, delicate girl at my table had gone through this.

She finally took a bite of lamb chop. "Not at first. You didn't get beaten unless you screwed up or tried to hide money instead of giving it to him. Some pimps use violence to control you right after they've turned you out. But be damned sure, violent or not, all pimps are in control, complete control. My pimp was always careful with me because I bruise easily and my body, my face was his fortune."

"I hate what happened to you," I said.

"So do I. My body was sold on the internet, in online classifieds, at strip clubs and sex parties, in malls and sports stadiums and..." she paused for a deep breath "...sometimes, on the street just like the olden days."

"How often?"

Rosie looked away. "Sometimes fifteen times a day."

The three of us sat in silence so deep, it attracted Charlie, who came over and put his head on my knee. Rosie pushed away her plate and regarded both of us. "Some of the girls in my group even forgot their real names and called themselves whatever their pimps had tattooed on them."

"Did any escape on their own?"

"It's hard, Red. Your pimp keeps close track of you. He decides where you live and with whom. He has older girls who keep track of you and discipline you if you try to run away. If you have a baby, he threatens to hurt the baby if you don't follow orders. He tells you what to wear, what to eat, when to go out to work. If you resist, he deprives you of food and sleep."

"And drugs?"

"My pimp not so much. He wanted me alert and sober so I could work hard. Other pimps did give out drugs and booze as rewards, but only when they could spare the girl for the few hours she was too high to perform."

"You stayed for two years. Why?" Joe's voice was soft but insistent.

"Didn't know where else to go." Rosie put down her fork and ran her fingers through her hair. Her blue eyes watered. "Until a good cop arrested me and sent me to sex trade rehab out of state." She pushed back her chair. "Even then, I ran away from rehab and turned a few tricks in Denver before I realized I didn't want to be on the street by myself."

I was incredulous. "You ran away and went back to it?"

Rosie nodded. "For a week, and then I got arrested again."

She turned to Joe. "I know it's difficult to understand, but selling myself was all I knew how to do. I didn't learn until months later that I had a mind as well as a body. And I'm not unusual, Joe. Even if you find Cathy, she may not come with you willingly. You may have to arrest her."

Chapter 5

Later that night, after Rosie had gone home, I lay in bed next to Joe. Neither of us had spoken since Rosie left, but we could read each other's thoughts. Then Joe spoke, his voice low and reasonable in the darkness. "You know why I have to do this, don't you?"

"I know. It's something about what happened in Chicago."

A sigh came from deep inside him. "You can't imagine what it's like to know you have accidentally killed a child."

He was right. I couldn't imagine it.

"That boy was just trying to get some money to help his mother. I think I told you I found out afterward that she had cancer and she was trying to raise the kid and his brothers on welfare."

"You told me. But you also told me the kid had dressed himself in that big coat and ski mask so the delicatessen clerk would think he was a grown man."

"I can still see that boy as clearly as I saw him then. I should have figured it out. It was eighty degrees outside and there was this guy in a big quilted coat and a wool ski mask. Later I figured out he was a boy trying to look like a grown man, trying to rob a store with an old gun he had found in an alley, a gun that didn't work. I can see his eyes through the hole in the mask, enormous and wet. I can see him pointing the gun at the clerk and then waving it at me. Jesus, Red, he was crying. I should have known he was just a kid trying to look big and terrifying. I should have known I didn't have to shoot him."

"Oh, Joe."

Another sigh. "And that goddamned gun. I should have known he wasn't a threat to me or the clerk."

"How could you have known?"

"By the way he was holding it. His hands were shaking so hard he could hardly keep a grip on it."

I put my hand over Joe's chest and my head on his shoulder. "My love, you know that's not rational. The fact that his hands were shaking didn't mean he wouldn't shoot. In fact, because he was so scared, he might have shot the gun accidentally and killed you or the clerk."

We lay in silence. A few minutes later, he said, "Since it happened, I've felt I don't deserve to have children of my own, but maybe if I could save another kid…"

My chest tightened. He sounded close to tears. I kissed his neck. "Tell me more about going undercover to infiltrate a trafficking ring. What's your plan? Or what's Reno's plan? How do you get even one of those girls safely out of there?"

Joe's voice was still strained in the darkness next to me. "I still have to work out some of the details with the Reno chief, but one idea we discussed was for me show up as a pimp who is looking for a girl who ran off with another pimp. A guy from Chicago who is willing to pay some big money to get the girl back from whoever is running her now."

"And you think you can penetrate a trafficking ring with that story?"

"It's not all that unusual. Occasionally a girl gets lured away by a rival pimp who promises her a bigger cut of the money and better treatment. Usually, if she's caught, the girl is beaten. But not killed. These guys are in it for money and that's what the girls mean to them."

"Any other ideas?"

"Sure. I may just get a job that puts me close to the action. Something in a bar or casino."

"Will you have to pose as a john?"

Joe's hand grasped mine. "That's probably not the best way. I need to be seen as someone who's willing to provide a girl, not as a customer."

"And if your cover gets blown?"

"Red, stop it. I'm good at this. Once I've gotten in with these people, I'm in and out fast."

"You better be. I will hate sleeping alone."

I felt his body turn and the warmth of his skin come over mine. "Me too."

Joe packed a small bag and left early the next morning to see his chief in Landry and then head to Reno. After a long and lingering kiss in the kitchen, he said, "Sweetheart, I promise I'll try to call every night if I can. But don't panic if I miss a night. Remember, I'll be passing as an angry pimp looking for his property or a new setup on Reno. I can't act like some happy guy with a beautiful girlfriend at home in Landry."

Right after he left, I threw up in the kitchen sink. I was sure I was sick with something, or else having an unpleasant version of an anxiety attack. I'd lived alone for much of my adult life, but the prospect of being without Joe for what could be two or three weeks not only made me nauseous but also depressed and irritable. A sad yearning filled my now empty stomach. I felt abandoned. Intellectually, I knew there was no reason. Joe had just gone on an undercover assignment. But I think the fact that he was going into danger heightened my anxiety and acute sense of loneliness.

As I washed my face, I realized I hadn't felt that kind of

loneliness since the day I went back to Ohio to commit my father to a hospital for Alzheimer's patients. It was the fall of my second year at Mountain West and the call came to me from his doctor. "Meredith, I'm sorry, but Thad should not live alone and he refuses to move to California to live with his sister."

Poor Evangeline. I was sure she had made a generous offer to keep her older brother, but how the hell was a busy professor with two kids and a husband supposed to care for a man with Alzheimer's? I knew she loved him as much as I did, but Thaddeus Solaris was no longer the man either of us had known and loved. He could not even remember our names.

I flew to Ohio and put my darling father, my champion and mentor, into a hospital. He had abandoned me for dementia just as my mother had abandoned me for whiskey.

I'd caught the next plane back to Nevada and, as we took off over the green farmlands of my childhood, I put my cheek against the cold airplane window. Goodbye, Ohio.

I gave Charlie one final pat and went out the back door. I got into my car and shook my head to clear the cobwebs. My father had died. Joe had taken over in my life as my faithful lover who would come home as soon as he could. I had Sadie and Phyllis and Nell as dear friends. I was certainly not alone. I had my job as dean and good work to do to keep me company. *Get a grip.*

But old memories persisted.

When I was in grammar school, my father had given me a small black dog, perhaps to make up for my mother's indifference as she lost herself in alcohol. I adored the dog, part spaniel and part who-knows-what, and named him Reggie. One bitter cold day in January, I came home and Reggie was nowhere. "Ran away," said my mother, well into an afternoon of boozy dimness.

"Ran away?" I screamed.

"That idiot delivery boy from the liquor store left the gate open and the stupid mutt ran away."

My father and I searched for Reggie for weeks. We drove all over the city. We registered with the Humane Society and called the county shelter twice a day. We made posters with pictures of Reggie's adorable puppy face and offered a reward of five hundred dollars. We put the posters up on trees, near schools, in bars and supermarkets. Everywhere. People called, "I think I saw your dog on my block. Three days ago." Three days ago. Jesus. But at least if he had been sighted, that gave us hope Reggie was still alive.

"I feel like I've lost a child," my father said, driving through the gloom of the Ohio winter. We had been searching for four freezing cold weeks. Snow was on the ground. I was sure my father thought the dog dead and gone, but we kept on looking every day because I became hysterical at the idea of us giving up. All I could think about was my beautiful little dog, hit by a car, or bitten by a larger dog and needing help, or picked up and kept by someone who didn't even bother to look at the tags on his collar. If Reggie was dead, I had to be sure. If taken, I had to take him back.

Four weeks and two days after Reggie ran away, we got a call from the caretaker of a cemetery ten miles away from our house.

"I got a little black dog here. Looks like the one on your poster. He's been chasing a rabbit around the gravestones. Pretty thin. But alive."

My father raced home from his last class at the university and drove like a madman to the cemetery. I wept the entire way. Reggie was alive.

"Four weeks lost in this weather? This dog's a friggin' miracle," said the caretaker when he handed Reggie over to us, a mass of shivering, dirty wet fur. A pink tongue emerged and licked my hand.

As I drove to the Mountain West campus, I thought of my father's unconditional love for me and his unfailing effort to search for Reggie. I took a deep breath and decided to snap out of it. If a small dog could live on rabbits and garbage through four winter weeks, a muscular six-foot-four detective should be able to make it through a two-week mission and come home safe. And I should be able to handle it and believe in his ability to survive whatever came his way.

I shook my head again to ward off the tears. Dammit. I must learn to become more of an optimist. Remember Reggie. Better yet, remember that you found Reggie and brought him home and he lived for sixteen years.

As soon as I got to my office, my first act was to call Sadie. "Can we move our lunch to today? I need a friend."

"Hold on a moment," was her response, and I could tell she was covering the receiver with her hand and talking to someone. Curious. Sadie lived alone. Who was there?

She came back on the line. "See you at noon. Everything all right?"

"Not really, but it's a long story. I'll tell you at Gormley's over a glass of wine or two." I hung up and turned to look out the window. The quad was turning a bright spring green and the trees were budding. But I was not cheered up.

"Two glasses of wine in the middle of the day? That doesn't sound good." Nell was behind me with the usual stack of papers to be dealt with that morning.

"You're probably right," I said. "I should stick to hot tea today."

"How's your stomach?"

"Still a bit queasy, but it got better yesterday afternoon, so I'm hoping I'll be fine later."

"Do you think you should see your doctor?"

"Maybe."

"Why don't I call her and see if I can get you in later today or tomorrow?"

"Thank you, Mother Nell."

Her protectiveness comforted me. Nell had not been all that warm to me when I had first come to the Journalism School at Mountain West, but since the death of the former dean, she had become a close friend as well as my assistant. Over time, I learned she had one son with a husband who had died when she was in her thirties, and that she had applied for her academic job as soon as her son could be left home by himself. Reserved and mousy when we first met, she had blossomed with the love of Wynan Congers, a former deputy police chief from Las Vegas. Since falling in love with him, Nell had become upbeat and vibrant and so thoughtful to the students and to me. I could only wish her all the luck in the world.

"How did the grade appeal go yesterday?"

"Edwin was tied up so I saw the student. He was sure the professor gave him a low grade because of the opinions he had expressed in his final essay last semester. I read through the essay he had written and pointed out a slew of spelling and grammatical errors, suggesting the low grade reflected the quality of his writing, not the merits of his opinion."

"Did he accept your judgment?"

"Not at first. For a while he insisted that his writing errors never counted for so much in his other courses. But then he relented when I explained that, in journalism courses—and in life—writing errors matter."

"Excellent. Is he one of our majors?"

"He was. But since we're so fussy and demanding, he's decided to switch his major to a less demanding discipline."

"Whatever that is." We both sighed.

Nell carefully arranged the stack of papers on my desk. "There's something else that won't help your stomach. You should probably take a look at the online student paper before you start in on the other stuff."

The headline took over the top of my computer screen. "White Supremacist to Speak at Purist Party." Below the headline was a picture of Danica Boerum behind a podium, right arm raised, fist clenched around a rifle in unabashed imitation of Charlton Heston addressing the NRA in 2000.

I scrolled down to find several other photos. Most were of the riots that had occurred at the other universities. One was of Boerum with her bodyguard towering over her. The man was standing with his back to the camera and described as Danica's constant watchdog. Reputed to weigh over two hundred and eighty pounds, the caption described him as a former professional wrestler.

The article was brief, but quoted two of the Mountain West faculty who were urging the university administration to ban Boerum's appearance. No direct quote from me, but a reference to journalism faculty who supported the Purists' right to invite any speaker they wanted to their own meeting.

"Perhaps you were never destined to have a moment's peace," said Sadie, draining her cup of black tea and giving me her best ironic smile. "Maybe it's your red hair. Just attracts trouble like static electricity."

Wilson, the owner of Gormley's, approached with a china teapot in his hands. Without asking her, he refilled Sadie's cup. "How about you, Red? Coffee, tea or wine?"

Mindful of my delicate stomach, I chose tea and a turkey sandwich.

Sadie looked sympathetic. "I've already had three calls this morning about Danica Boerum, and I'm retired. I can't imagine how many calls you and the administration have gotten."

"Too many. I haven't had as many as Manny Lorenzo, but I have a stack of messages on my desk, a screen full of emails and a meeting with students scheduled for this afternoon."

Sadie sat back in her chair, letting the dim overhead lamp illuminate her thick white hair. Unlike Danica Boerum's cropped cut, Sadie's hair was long and in a loose bun at the nape of her neck. It curled softly around her face, and I often had to resist the impulse to put my hand on her head and pet her as I would a beautiful cat.

After one of her thoughtful pauses, she said, "You're going to have to be careful of this, you know. Everyone will expect you to be a good First Amendment liberal and defend Boerum's right to speak."

"I sense a 'but...'"

"No 'but' to your defense, but there's been a growing tendency in several departments on campus, and at other universities, to protect students from speech that offends, hurts feelings, raises memories of abuse, etcetera."

"I know. Manny and I were just on that subject. People call them 'triggers.' I worry we try to protect students too much. College is supposed to be a place where you encounter upsetting ideas and theories. And learn to deal with them."

Sadie nodded. "I'm with you. I think we infantilize students when we protect them from events and ideas they may abhor but should know about. Nonetheless..."

"Nonetheless, I could get on the wrong side of a number of faculty, not to mention students, who will accuse me of defending the indefensible."

"As noted, no peace for you, my friend." She took another sip. "Now, how goes it with you and Joe?"

Sadie loved Joe almost as much as I did. She may have been

seventy, but she still had an eye for a man with a strong face and broad shoulders. Especially one who told her jokes and enchanted her by reciting poetry from memory. Sadie's favorite poet was William Blake, and Joe had surprised her by knowing most of Blake's major works. Some by heart.

"Joe's fine, but gone for two weeks or so."

"Oh?"

"I have a student who wanted his help finding her cousin who is being trafficked by a pimp in Reno."

"Naturally Joe said yes."

"Naturally, and more than that, he's agreed to help the Reno police by going undercover to penetrate one of the sex-trafficking rings that infest tourist destinations like Reno. You have to keep all this a secret, you know."

"Of course. I always keep your secrets. And his. Sex trafficking. How painful. And Joe undercover and away for two weeks. How depressing. And scary."

"Sadie, I am absolutely terrified of what he's trying to do. Traffickers are often ex-drug dealers, and we know what they do to anyone they suspect of betrayal. Those photographs from villages in Latin America..."

"Stop it. You'll make both of us sick."

Chapter 6

I left Sadie having a third cup of tea with Wilson and walked back to my office. Gormley's was just off the west side of Mountain West campus and a short distance from the journalism school. I savored my campus treks as the time I had to myself. Time to think things through. Sadie was right. Joe's mission was dangerous, but somehow I felt better just for having shared my fear with her. All in all, life was good, and once again, I resolved to stop conjuring up potential tragedy.

Back in my office, I checked my cell phone. Damn, a message from Joe. He had called during my lunch with Sadie. "Probably won't call again tonight. Reno PD has set me up with a job as a pit boss at a local casino where I might run into my targets. Please don't call my cell. I love you."

I love you too, I said to the window and the trees outside. I love your long beautiful body and your dark green eyes and the rare off-kilter smile that takes over your face. I love your caring so much about those young girls that you are willing to put your own important work on hold and go to another city to help out.

Nell entered with a tray of soft drinks. I turned from the window, hoping she could not read my melancholy. But she just smiled and worked her particular magic at dragging me back into the present. "We're expecting a dozen or so students in a few minutes to discuss the Purist meeting. Leaders from the j-school and some from the university Student Council."

As if on cue, one stood in my doorway. Rosie Jenkins.

"I don't have any news from Joe," I said as she made her way to the couch.

"I understand. It's too soon. I'm just grateful he's on the job. Anyway, I'm here for the meeting on Danica Boerum." She scrunched her face up. "The more research I do on that woman the more I think she's nothing like the bitch I knew in LA. She's too straitlaced and much too conservative. Also, she speaks with a soft voice and the women pimps I knew in LA were all shouters."

"I didn't think there were any women pimps."

"Oh, yeah. Some of the meanest pimps around are women. They usually have no sexual interest in the girls so they're all business and discipline. The woman whose eyes remind me of Danica's started out as a bottom bitch. Then her pimp got killed and she took over his business in LA and later in Vegas."

"Vegas?" said Nell. "I wonder if Wynan ever ran into her."

"C'mon, you two. We're talking about Danica Boerum's political horror show. Let's not digress into a discussion of sex trafficking."

"You're right. Except that I find both of them equally hateful," said Rosie. "The woman I remember from LA was younger and had long black hair, not white. But those eyes do get to me. There's something familiar." Rosie giggled. "Maybe they're related. Do you think maybe Danica Boerum might have had a younger sister who strayed off the proper Purist reservation and went over to the dark side?"

"Boerum's already on the dark side as far as I'm concerned," said Nell.

Five students arrived at the same time and took seats in chairs around my office. A moment later, another group of six walked in. Nell had been right. A dozen squeezed into my sofa and chairs or sat on the floor. The president of the student council, a tall doe-eyed boy with a soft southern accent, spoke first. "Dean Solaris, we've talked to the provost and he's said he doesn't plan to ban Danica Boerum's appearance next week, and that you agree with him."

"I do."

"We believe in free speech too, but we're really worried. We were hoping we could persuade you to change your mind. And that you could change the provost's mind." A slight frown creased his brow.

"I doubt I can change Manny Lorenzo's mind about anything, much less this."

An African-American girl I recognized as one of my ethics students two years ago raised her hand. "The thing is, we have minority students on campus who are already planning protests..."

Another girl sitting on the couch next to Rosie interrupted, "And some are football players who are always ready for a fight. I mean big guys who like to mess it up." She made two fists and simulated boxing moves in the air.

I took a deep breath and moved closer to my desk. "I understand why you've come to me about this, but I still believe that the Purists have a right to invite their own speaker to their own party. And I'm sure the provost told you he plans tight security."

A tall boy with a shock of blond hair spilling onto his forehead stood up from the other end of the couch. "We all support free speech and the First Amendment, but we also want a safe campus." He rubbed what were probably sweaty palms on his jeans. "Believe me, Dean Solaris, if this woman starts mouthing her racist bullshit, private party or no, we'll have serious trouble. We may not be allowed to carry guns on campus, but most of my fraternity brothers own guns and they'll bring them to the speech. You can be damn sure."

Guns. Good Lord.

"You know that's against the law."

"We all know it. But, c'mon, this is Nevada, and it's legal for us to keep guns at home. Most of these guys do and many live very near campus. I mean, we're talking a block away from the Purists' party."

Visions of the riot at an east coast campus last year began to form in my mind. And that particular riot had happened in a New England state that had strict gun control laws. If memory served, three students and one police officer had been shot and knives and rocks had wounded many more.

"Why can't you persuade your friends not to go? If no one shows up except a small group of Purists, there will be no violence."

The tall blond boy again. "Because this is our campus..."

A girl on the side of the room. "Yeah, and if some students have a right to sponsor a racist, we have the right to sponsor a protest and shout them down."

The student council president raised and lowered his hand, signaling the room to calm down. "Look, the point is we can't persuade people not to go. Too many are already heated up about this. Some are spoiling for a fight. At the very least the Purists should be forced to move the party to an off-campus location, some meeting room in town..."

Rosie looked up from her notebook. "Or better yet, some other town. Reno has a lot of places they could rent."

Nervous laughter.

Then it was so quiet you could hear the trees rustling outside my window.

I leaned against my desk. "I'll talk to the provost again, but I don't think either of us will change on this."

Someone groaned.

I stood up straight. "Look, you are the leaders of the

students on this campus and you may have much more persuasive power than you realize. You also have as much responsibility for student conduct and student safety as the administration does. Why don't you hold a rally *before* the Purist party? Urge common sense. Tell your friends that if they go, they should keep absolutely silent. Silence can be a powerful rebuke to a speaker who expects response, even negative response."

The disappointment on their faces told me what they thought of that idea. They solemnly filed toward the door, dutifully dumping their soda cans in the wastebasket Nell had put by the door. Good people. Righteous kids. Damn, I wished I had a better message for them.

Rosie stayed behind. "I'm thinking of trying for a phone interview with Boerum this week. Any helpful hints?"

"Not right now. But if you get the interview and want to call me before publishing, I would gladly be your editor."

Rosie smiled. "My editor? Or my censor? You just want to be sure I don't publish anything that starts this firestorm sooner."

"I'm as scared as they are," said Manny an hour later when I reached him by phone. "And actually, since our talk, I have approached the student leaders of the Purists and asked if they would consider moving to an off-campus venue."

"And the answer was…"

"A ten-minute diatribe on their First Amendment rights plus my cowardice at being unwilling to defend them against their fellow students."

"Well, their house is on our campus."

"Indeed, and I got an earful about another student group inviting Michael Moore here five years ago even though some major donors had vigorously objected and threatened to stop donating."

"I remember that. Moore came, spoke to a raucous crowd and left without any serious problems. We did lose one donor who insisted to the end that we were all Communist sympathizers, but the others hung in there. Grudgingly, perhaps."

"Let's hope we survive Danica Boerum." I heard him sigh. "Did they really say some students might bring guns to campus?"

Chapter 7

I slept badly that night. A spring rainstorm was howling outside my window and shaking the climbing rose trellis below. Joe's phone call had come in late, brief and uninformative. No news, good or bad. In addition to my anxiety for him, I worried about the student prediction for guns and violence. I felt sorry for Manny and Fred Stoddard, the university president. I suspected their phones had been ringing most of the evening.

By six o'clock in the morning I gave up and decided to watch the sun rise, feed Charlie and then go to see my doctor who had agreed to a seven-thirty appointment. My stomach was still bothering me, and I wanted to be sure it was not some flu bug instead of stress brought on by the prospect of bloodshed on my campus. Charlie was thrilled with an earlier-than-usual bowl of chow, but breakfast for me was out of the question. My one cup of coffee barely stayed down as I walked to my car.

It was still unseasonably warm and the night's rain had left a trace of humidity in our normally dry high desert air. A lilac near my garage had started to bloom. I held my breath to avoid the heavy fragrance I usually cherished. I thought it might aggravate the instability in my stomach.

I drove carefully, trying hard not to ruin my car's upholstery. Traffic was still light before normal work hours began. The air was clear and cool and I opened the car window and inhaled the freshness of it. The sky was bright with Nevada's pale morning light that silhouetted the buildings of Landry. My doctor's office was in a low building near the hospital. Hers was the only office lit up when I parked my car.

Helen Ferguson, M.D. and personal savior, had seen me through two horrid bouts of flu and a bad case of shingles my third year of teaching. She was, as they say, built like a Sherman tank—short, wide-shouldered, no fat and all muscle. She kept her hair gray, short and spiky. Low maintenance to allow more time for recreation. When Helen wasn't practicing medicine, she was hiking our mountains, skiing, working out at the gym or leaving us for weeks to go endurance riding in some unheard of part of the world. Nothing fazed Helen.

After a thorough exam, I sat in her office looking at framed color photographs of Lake Tahoe and awaiting her diagnosis.

She came in, took off her glasses and gazed at me as she sat down behind her desk. Helen had enormous eyes, so soft they belied her straightforward, sometimes gruff approach. "I think you know what your problem is," she began.

"I keep throwing up, or wanting to."

"Every morning." She put her chin on her hands and the edge of her mouth curled ever so slightly

I nodded, fighting a new wave of nausea.

"Red, you're old enough and smart enough to figure out what's happening to your own body."

Another wave, accompanied by a cold sweaty feeling at the back of my neck.

Helen laughed. "You're pregnant."

"What?"

"Not by much. I would guess about six to eight weeks, but I should run some tests to be certain."

I was out of my chair like a shot and across the room away from her. I braced my hands against the wall and stared into a photograph of a Lake Tahoe beach, a close-up of the water's edge. It was as if I hoped the clarity of the rocks and sand under the water would restore some sense to me. I turned around.

"Oh, Helen. This can't be right. I'm so careful. I never forget."

Helen put her glasses back on and looked at her desk. "Well, sometimes we don't remember what we forgot."

Pregnant. Oh my God.

"What do you want to do about this, Red?"

"What do you mean?"

Helen pushed her glasses farther up her nose. "I mean it's still early enough in the pregnancy to terminate if you don't want this baby."

I think it was the word "baby" that sent a shock wave through me. I realized I was no longer nauseous. Now I was trembling. A baby? Did I want children? Yes, someday, particularly now that Joe and I were happy together. But I wanted to plan for them, make sure my job schedule could be accommodated. No ambivalence on his part or mine. Absolute certainty. Not a surprise. And certainly not an accident.

Helen sat patiently waiting for me to speak. Minutes passed. My brain exploded with visions and then the words that came out of my mouth surprised me. I stuttered, "Terminate? No." My mind was racing. "I think…I think what I want…is to have this baby."

Helen sat back and clasped her hands. The muscles around her mouth kept on moving. "You're sure?"

"Yes."

"Good. At your age I don't know how easy it may be for you to get pregnant later on. So, my friend, if you want to have a child, now is probably a good time."

I must have looked stupid staring at her. "I'm not married."

"So what?" She stretched her remarkably muscular

forearms across her desk. "Lots of unmarried women have babies these days. Some quite deliberately. You have a good income and you're a sensible, healthy woman. Is the father a reliable fellow?"

Oh my God, reliable? What would Joe think of this? The only times we had ever talked about children, including the night before he left, he had said that he wasn't sure he deserved children or that fate should ever let him become a father. I had dismissed it as an overreaction on his part, but what if he really meant it?

"He's a good man," I said, feebly.

"Well, if he's a good man, he'll get used to the idea and may even propose marriage, or at least be generous with child support. You should tell him, you know. In my opinion, he's entitled to that."

"I know."

I dimly remember Helen giving me a prescription for vitamins, a directive to limit caffeine to two coffees a day and a perfunctory hug as I left the office in a daze. I knew I was in no shape to go to work, so I headed for the one person, other than Joe, I knew I could trust.

Sadie's house was a single-story brick cottage on the edge of Landry. Large pots lined the edge of her paved driveway. The fat green noses of hyacinths were sticking up ready to release their color and fragrance.

At nine in the morning, Sadie would just have gotten up for breakfast and was probably sitting in her kitchen drinking coffee. I went around to the back of the house. The lilac by her back door was in fuller bloom than mine, but the smell didn't make me dizzy.

What did make my head spin was the sight of the figure

that opened the back door. Wilson McCarthy, owner of Gormley's, dressed in a t-shirt and pajama pants.

"Good morning, Red," he said, with more cheerfulness than I had ever heard in his usually cynical voice. "Come on in."

I'm sure my jaw was still hanging open as I walked into Sadie's kitchen and sat down at her table. "I didn't know you and Sadie were…"

"Close," he said pouring a cup of coffee. "If memory serves you like a little milk in this."

I shook my head. "Just half a cup, black please," I said.

He handed me the cup and smiled. Broadly. I had never seen Wilson smile broadly. He hardly smiled at all in Gormley's. His humor was famously cynical. This gentler and much cheerier version of Wilson would take some getting used to.

"How long have you and Sadie…"

"A month and a week," said a woman's voice behind me.

I turned. Sadie was in the doorway dressed in an elegant blue satin robe, her white hair loose and tumbling over her shoulders. Her face was smooth with sleep but her cheeks were pink. With embarrassment at my intrusion?

I stammered, "Why didn't you say something to me? Why didn't you tell me about you two?"

Sadie smiled at Wilson and the look between them lasted for several seconds. "I was enjoying the secret of it," she said.

"Nonsense," said Wilson, leaning against the refrigerator. "She just wasn't sure things were going to work out between us."

I scrutinized him. Long-legged, lean with a well-muscled chest and arms. Good face with fine features, gray hair, rimless glasses that made him look scholarly. Yes, Wilson McCarthy was attractive. I wondered why I had never noticed before.

Sadie sat down and covered my hand with her. "I'm sorry, dear Red. I just wanted to be sure about this. Actually, I haven't told anyone yet, and you would have been the first."

I squeezed her hand. "Well, whatever this is, it's most becoming. You look very pretty this morning."

Wilson pushed off from the refrigerator and headed for the door. "I think I'll leave you ladies alone." He patted my shoulder on his way out. "So the dean of journalism can ask all those inappropriate questions that are flooding her mind."

I still held Sadie's hand. "Does your son know?"

Sadie got up and went to the coffee pot. "I haven't told him yet. Although I think his wife suspects something. I invited Wilson over for dinner last week when Bill and Nancy were visiting. My daughter-in-law is a shrewd observer."

"Why were you worried this wouldn't work? Everyone knows Wilson's had a thing for you for years."

Sadie sighed and returned to her chair. "Wilson's younger than I am. By several years."

"That's not necessarily a bad thing."

A dreamy smile. "No. Not at all."

I cleared my throat. "I take it he is in good health."

"He's in excellent health."

"Sadie, your eyes are twinkling."

"Yes. That happens rather frequently now."

"Oh, honey. This is good news. You should tell your kids. You should tell the world."

Her eyes took on a faraway gaze as she looked out the window. "I never thought I'd love another man after Jed died. And I'm still timid about it. Love among the ruins, you know."

"Love whenever it happens is wonderful."

"Yes, but the thought of sexual love involving people my age makes the children shudder."

"They'll get over it. I'm so happy for you."

"Thank you, Red." Her gaze returned to me. "But I've been so distracted I forgot to ask what brings you here so early in the morning. You usually call before."

"Sorry to barge in unannounced, but I have some news of my own I needed to tell you about."

"You have my full attention."

I sat back and took a final sip of coffee and a deep breath. Sadie's face turned from radiant to concerned.

"I'm going to have a baby."

Her hands flew up in the air. "A baby? Jesus, Mary and Joseph. I'm thrilled. When?"

"October or November. Dr. Ferguson isn't sure yet. She needs to do more tests."

Sadie got up and wrapped her arms around me and kissed my forehead. "A baby for the holidays. Oh, Red. This is terrific. How did Joe take the news?"

I felt my eyes tear up. "I haven't told him yet."

"Ah. That's right. Joe's gone undercover in Reno."

"I haven't seen him for days, and I never know when or if he's going to call at night."

Sadie took my hand again. "Oh, darling. You can't tell him this news over the phone. And certainly not while he's in the middle of a dangerous investigation. You'll have to wait until he's back and then pick a time when the two of you are alone in some peaceful place."

"I agree. But I'm really nervous about telling him at all."

"Really, why? Joe's great with kids. He's marvelous with his niece and nephew. I think he'll be delirious you're having his baby."

"I don't know about that. Remember the kid in Chicago?"

"The one he shot by accident?"

"That preys on Joe's mind. He said not long ago that he still feels so guilty he doesn't think he deserves to father a child of his own."

An awkward quiet settled over both of us. Sadie got up again and poured more coffee. She brought a container of milk over to the table. "Do you want something to eat for breakfast?"

"I'm afraid I usually lose my breakfast now."

"Try some saltines and club soda or ginger ale. That worked for me. And this will pass after the first trimester."

My eyes watered up again and this time the tears flowed. "Oh God. I'm a mess. I'm so frightened. I'm so scared Joe won't want me to have this baby." I grabbed her hand again. "But I've made up my mind. I am going to have this baby, no matter what he says."

Sadie pulled some tissues out of her pocket and handed them to me. Through my sniffling, I kept on. "When Ferguson said the word baby, I actually had a vision of one. In my arms. Looking up at me. Chubby legs moving. Tiny fingers around one of mine. Little bubbles between its lips. Dammit, Sadie. I saw myself with this child, and I knew I wanted it more than anything in the world."

Sadie almost whispered, "Then you shall have this child. Trust me, you will adore it and you will raise it beautifully. I am here for you. And, sooner or later, I think Joe will come around and be here for you too."

I blew my nose. "But you're not certain about Joe, are you?"

Sadie turned her head and her gaze returned to the window. "One can never be certain about another's feelings."

Chapter 8

I never thought of myself as needing family, but as I drove away from Sadie's, all I could think of was that I was an orphan, a pregnant orphan with no mother to hover over me and give me advice and no father to hug me and tell me he was delighted to become a grandparent. Thank God for Sadie. But I needed more. Especially with my uncertainty about Joe's reaction. Especially with Joe away.

When I got to my house I looked up the number of my father's sister. Evangeline Solaris Mulgrew lived in Sacramento where she taught physics at Sacramento State. She was younger than my father, and, although they had been devoted to each other when they were young and in college, the two had never spent much time together after my parents married. Evangeline and my mother, Emily, didn't get along, and Ohio was far enough away from California to guarantee little family contact. But Evangeline was my only living relative and would be my child's great-aunt.

I left a message on her office phone and went in search of some salted crackers and ginger ale. I called Nell and told her I would be out of the office for the day and to forward any call from Joe to my cell, but otherwise to please leave me alone to rest up from what I described as flu.

Half an hour later, Evangeline returned my call. She was

surprised to hear from me but pleased when I asked if I could drive to Sacramento and talk to her.

"Come to the house," she said. "I've finished my last class for today, and I'll make us a late lunch so we can catch up. It will be great to see you, Meredith. It's been at least three years since I visited you there. I'm dying to hear all about your new job as dean."

The drive gave me time to think about the incredible events of the morning and the views of the Sierra offered by Interstate 80 made me realize how fortunate I was to live in a beautiful part of the world. The rain we had gotten in the valley surrounding Landry had turned to snow in the higher elevations. Enormous evergreens grew out of thick white blankets. As I passed by the summit and a glistening Donner Lake, I realized how much I wished Joe were beside me. Much as I wanted him to find Rosie's cousin, I wanted him with me when I told my aunt I was pregnant. I wanted her to admire and congratulate him. I wanted her to meet the man I had finally found to love.

The tall pines and the bright sky reminded me of the weekends Joe and I had spent in the mountains at his parents' cottage. Those were the times we had talked about what mattered most to us. Not his work as a detective or mine as an educator, but our childhood memories, the people we had loved and lost. That's when Joe had opened up about the loss of his best friend, Charlie, who died in an automobile accident in his senior year of college. Charlie had inspired the name of our Golden Retriever.

That was the time I had confessed my hatred for my mother's drinking and what her disease had done to me and to my father—my wonderful, imaginative father who had perished in the maelstrom of Alzheimer's.

That's when Joe and I had first begun to talk about the

troubles in our parents' marriages and our own doubts and insecurities about ever being good at sustaining long-term relationships. We had tried so hard to reassure each other. We were falling in love and wanted ours to be a perfect union in spite of the odds against us.

The red dirt cliffs of Auburn, California came into view as the road began to descend. The snow disappeared as the air warmed. California's deciduous trees were starting to bud. I should have felt elated by the sight, but my mind stayed on Joe and his ever-present and unrelenting uncertainty.

Evangeline's house was set back from the street in the old part of Sacramento. She had been widowed for several years and her children were grown and gone, so she had moved to a small house with a white fence around a green lawn. She greeted me at the door looking so much like my dead father that my chest contracted. She was tall and slim just as he had been and her hair matched his graying brown. But it was the set of her mouth and the lines around her eyes that most reminded me of the first man I had ever adored.

She led me through the house, past a short hall lined with photographs of her family and a few of my father and me when we were all much younger. Her kitchen was large and painted yellow with white trim and white cabinets. Evidence of her interest in good cooking was everywhere I looked: bookshelves holding cookbooks and casseroles and skillets hanging over the sink. This was the kind of kitchen Joe would love, and Evangeline was the kind of serious, elegant woman he would enjoy knowing if they ever met.

The kitchen door opened to a sunny patio where she had set up a table under an umbrella. "Meredith, my darling, it's so good to see you. It's been much too long."

We sat and sipped lemonade. I picked at the pretty fruit salad she had made and we talked about the life of an academic. "I'm so proud you have been made dean of your school," she said. "Your father would have been over the moon about your success. I so wish he'd lived to see it."

"I'm not sure he would have understood much about my academic career. He seemed pleased when I left journalism for grad school and later when Mountain West offered me a job, but Dad didn't even know who I was the last few times I saw him."

"I know. Alzheimer's can be crueler to the family than the patient. But, Meredith, an additional cruelty is that sometimes the patients know more and feel more than we realize. I promise you, your father loved you with all his heart even as his mind failed him, even if he couldn't articulate it."

"Oh, I don't know about 'all his heart.' I think the lion's share of his heart went to my mother."

Evangeline frowned. "Probably not. You were the light of his life. Your mother, I fear, was more the bane of his existence."

That confused me. "How can you say that, Evangeline? My father dedicated his life to my mother, to finding a cure for her alcoholism. His love for her was overwhelming."

Evangeline cocked her head and her mouth formed a slight bitter smile. "For Thad I fear it was not so much love as penance."

"Penance?"

She rose. "Wait a minute, there's something I want to show you."

She left me on her patio with the sun warming the blossoms around me.

When she returned, Evangeline held a framed photograph in her hand. "Thad made me swear never to tell you this, but I think it's important you understand how he really felt." Evangeline ran her fingers over her hair and took a deep breath.

Then she handed me the photograph of three people standing under a tree. A young Evangeline next to a young and very handsome Thaddeus Solaris and a beautiful blond woman I had never seen before.

Evangeline put her hand over mine. "Before he got his doctorate, your father was deeply in love with another grad student at his university. She was a gorgeous Ph.D. candidate in Literature, and they were planning to get teaching jobs at the same university. I always hoped they would marry."

I stared at the photo. The woman next to my father with her arm around his waist was stunning. But it was the expression on my father's face that shocked me the most. I had never seen such joy in his eyes and his smile.

"What happened to her?"

Evangeline sighed and sat back in her chair. "One evening Thad and his beloved quarreled and she broke up their relationship. In despair, your father went to a bar, where he encountered Emily. They got drunk together and she invited him to her home. Their one-night stand left her pregnant with you."

So, I was not the only woman in my family to get pregnant by accident and outside of marriage.

I was astonished to learn my mother had not been the love of my father's life. "I never knew he had loved another woman."

"No, you didn't, but I did. She was terrific and just right for your father. However, despite my pleas and my frequently spoken misgivings, your father insisted upon doing the decent thing. Thad never tried to reconcile with his one true love. He married Emily."

"I always thought he worshipped my mother. Drunk or sober."

Evangeline looked grim. "I assure you he never worshipped your mother. He felt obligated to care for her. He seemed convinced her drinking was caused by their required marriage. After you were born, you became the light of his life. He adored you. You centered him, Meredith. You gave him hope even during his darkest times with Emily."

How about that? Here I had thought for years that, when it came to my father's love, I came in second. And then, just as I had with Sadie, I burst into tears. I wept not only for myself but also for my father, who had given up his happiness to raise me and take care of my dreadful mother.

My aunt was a good listener. I told her I was pregnant and talked nonstop for an hour, finally getting to the core of my anguish. "I'm not sure I will know how to be a good mother. Mine didn't set a very good example."

"No, she didn't. I sometimes wished I had found a way to make friends with your mother, but I loathed her drinking and her selfishness. If I hadn't disliked her so much, I could have spent more time with you. You were such a sweet, bright little girl, and it was clear you were lonely. Even your father couldn't make up for those hours when he was working and away."

"I worry I won't be any good at raising a child."

That brought a smile back to her face. "Don't worry, Meredith. You are a strong, intelligent, rather remarkable woman. You'll be a great mother. Now tell me more about the man responsible for this happy event."

So I told her about Joe and how he was smart and kind and good-looking and brave. But I left out the part about wondering how he would take the news of the baby and whether or not he would stick around.

Evangeline invited me to stay the night, but I knew I had to get back to school, and I wanted to be there for Rosie if she needed me. I drove back over the mountains just as the sun was setting and the late spring dusk was silhouetting the trees against the sky.

When I entered my empty house, my mood had shifted and I found myself experiencing an unexpected sense of optimism. Sadie and Evangeline were wise women and they were both right. I was going to be fine. With or without Joe, I would get through this pregnancy. My father had once said, "Never be afraid to do what you truly want to do. Plant your garden, write your book, take your trip, have your child."

I could almost hear his voice in my mind until a short sharp bark intruded. Charlie was hungry and I was late.

I filled his bowls and made myself a sandwich and a glass of milk. "No more red wine for me. Not for months." Charlie pretended attentiveness.

After supper, I went to my home computer to tackle what I figured was a day's worth of unanswered emails. Several complaints about Boerum's appearance, plus a few about the deans' meeting work. Just as I was about to put the screen to sleep, a final email popped up. It was from Rosie Jenkins. I read it, then read it again:

"Red, I interviewed Danica Boerum over the phone this afternoon. Tomorrow I'll send a draft for you to look at. She was very formal with me and not especially open or articulate, so I tried something to shake her up a bit at the end. I asked her if she had ever lived in LA and she said, 'No, why do you ask?' I said she reminded me of a woman with long black hair I had known in my old neighborhood a few years ago, and I wondered if she had a relative there. She hung up on me. I don't know what that means, but I guess I said something pretty stupid."

I sat back in my chair and felt my earlier optimism drain away. Oh, Rosie, you sure did say something stupid. You effectively asked a dangerous woman if she was related to a sex trafficker.

Chapter 9

Nell was waiting in my office the next morning, excited about finally finding a place to hold her wedding. So absorbed in her good news she didn't even ask how I was feeling or how things had gone at my doctor's appointment.

"It's just beautiful, Red. And the courtyard will be wonderful in October with all the maples in orange and red."

October. When the baby was likely due. But Joe still didn't know and it was too soon to tell Nell or any friends other than my dear wise women. Wait until the end of the first trimester before you tell the world, Helen had advised. Just to be sure.

I told Nell I was happy she had found her wedding site. She held a folder out to me. "Remember, you're meeting with the Faculty Senate at ten. Here's the report you wanted me to type up."

I took the folder. "You haven't seen Rosie Jenkins around here, have you?"

"No. Were you expecting her?"

"She emailed me last night. I emailed back and called her once last night and again this morning. No luck."

I thumbed through the folder, checked my messages and tried to focus on my report to the Senate. Each semester it was the custom of the Senate to invite the dean of each of the colleges to attend a meeting and give a progress report on the activities and coming events the college planned.

My thoughts kept drifting back to Rosie. I left my desk and went into Nell's office. "While I'm at the Senate meeting, could you please see if you can track Rosie down? I really need to talk to her as soon as possible."

The Mountain West Faculty Senate met in a large conference room on the third floor of the library. Through the tall windows overlooking the campus, I could see the snow still on the tops of the Sierra against a bright cloudless sky.

Shelby Vane, a friend and ally, had recently been elected Chair of the Senate. He lumbered into view as I entered the conference room and stared at the scene outside. Shelby's rumpled features formed a warm smile and his big arms went around me for a hug. "Ah, Queen Red, my favorite dean," he murmured into my ear. "So good to see you."

I kissed his cheek and returned the hug. "How's life at the top of the Senate?"

"Bureaucratic," he said leading me farther into the room. "When it's not hopelessly political." Shelby and I had served on a quarrelsome committee last year formed to improve the university's procedures for sexual assault. He had also helped Joe, Wynan and me search for a missing student. I had grown fond of him.

He escorted me to a seat at an enormous round table. Thirty faculty senators either stood chatting or sat reading notes around the circular mahogany table that had a hole in the middle making it into an enormous "O." Inside the circle was a smaller round table holding audiovisual equipment. The table shape, resembling those used for diplomatic conferences, had been designed for the Senate and was intended to make sure no one senator seemed more important than any other.

I waited patiently through ten minutes of Senate business,

and then Shelby introduced me. I stood with notes in hand, but it was only a second or two before it became clear the Mountain West senators were not the least bit interested in the doings of the journalism school. Danica Boerum was on the minds of all in the room.

Shelby recognized a senator from Economics, no doubt a pal of Bridget's. "So, Dr. Solaris, we hear you are in favor of a white supremacist bigot speaking on this campus. We appreciate journalism's defense of free speech. God knows we need it in our classrooms. But really, Danica Boerum? Isn't that going too far?"

I put down my notes and adopted my most patient and conciliatory tone. My questioner was known as a provocateur. "I'm not in favor of her opinions. I'm just not opposed to allowing her to speak. What I'm in favor of is the First Amendment."

Another senator rose, reading from a document, "Have you read the Purist manifesto? Listen to this: 'Article One: We believe that the United States originated under European civilization and that the American people and government should remain European. We adamantly oppose the immigration of non-European and non-Western peoples, enforced if necessary by placing troops on our national borders. We believe that non-Europeans already in America should be encouraged to return to their own countries...'" He looked up from the document. "Need I go on?"

Shelby interrupted, "Tom, I think we are all well aware of the Purist beliefs."

Undeterred, the senator flipped to another page of the document. "How about this then? 'Article Twelve: We also oppose all efforts to mix the races'...or 'Article Fifteen: We oppose the destruction of the American family through toleration of interracial marriage and homosexuality...'" The man's face was turning purple. "Those are fighting words and should be banned from this campus."

Shelby interrupted again, "Tom, we invited the Dean of Journalism here to speak to us about her school. Are we going to let her talk?"

The man sat down, still huffing as if he had climbed three flights of stairs.

"Not if she supports that garbage," said a woman sitting next to him.

I took a breath and began, "I don't support any of the Purist philosophy, nor am I the least bit happy about Boerum's impending appearance and the publicity it seems to have generated."

The room quieted down but murmuring continued.

"Senators, this is a university. We believe in freedom of expression. We debate ideas here. We cherish our ability and our willingness to disagree. We encourage our students to examine ideas and theories that make them uncomfortable."

The murmuring came to a stop and then started again.

An older senator from across the room spoke up. "What if the ideas make them more than uncomfortable? What if the ideas dredge up painful memories from someone's childhood?" I thought about my friend, Phyllis Baker, whom I had not spoken to since our encounter in the elevator.

A young female senator chimed in, "What if the ideas make them feel diminished or hurt and angry?"

I took a deep breath. "I grant you, there are a number of ideas that make me very angry. But I'm not sure suppressing them, much less pretending they don't exist, is the way to go. Our students need to examine even the most hateful ideas while they are here in our classrooms, where it's safe to examine and argue about them. We do them no favors when we send them into a world of cruel and stupid ideas they have never encountered. They need to be armed with information and critical analytic abilities."

An African-American woman sitting next to Shelby raised her hand. Her nameplate identified her as Dr. Thea Gray, Vice Chairman of the Senate. "I think Dean Solaris is right. We should give our students more credit. They are stronger than we may think. We're worrying—I know I have been worrying—too much about the effect Boerum's speech might have on our community."

"Perhaps the major effect it will have is to bring us closer together," said a senator near me.

Dr. Gray again, "Even if it doesn't, Boerum's dogmatism may give us an opportunity to teach a pertinent lesson about the value of diversity and the true events of American history."

"Yes, we can put some focus on those nasty quarrels between the Founding Fathers," said a history professor nearby.

But the woman next to the economics senator would not be quieted. "Teaching moments be damned. I still think we should have a motion to request the president ban Boerum's appearance on campus. Let them listen to her somewhere else."

"So moved."

This called for a vote.

"I think we should do this by secret ballot," said the economics professor.

That chewed up another half hour. In the end, the motion did not carry, and after a little grumbling, Shelby said, "Are we now ready to listen to the dean's report on the School of Journalism? She's been waiting patiently for over an hour."

After my report, the senate recessed for ten minutes. Shelby headed over as I was leaving. Another hug. He whispered in my ear, "Nice work, lady. That vote might have been much closer without you here. In my opinion, the Red Queen rules."

*   *   *

Nell was waiting for me in the hallway outside the Senate conference room. Her face was ashen and her hands were clenched against her chest. "Oh, Red, I'm afraid I have bad news. Rosie's in the hospital."

"What? Why?"

"She was shot last night. She's barely alive and they don't know if she'll recover."

Nell held out my car keys. I grabbed them and raced out of the building to the journalism parking lot. I drove like a madwoman to the Landry hospital.

I made it to the hospital in ten minutes, parked illegally and raced through the double doors. I was frantic with worry and the nurse at the emergency desk was much too calm. "Are you a relative?" she said quietly after I had almost shouted Rosie's name.

"I'm her guardian," I lied.

"One moment," said the nurse in her infuriatingly even tones. She reached for her telephone and took forever to punch in three numbers. "I'll call the doctor."

I paced the floor until a thin woman in green scrubs appeared in the waiting room. "Dr. Solaris?"

"Is Rosie Jenkins alive?"

"Yes. But she's critical. She was beaten and shot twice in the abdomen."

"Will she live?"

"We've removed the bullets and her major organs seem to be intact, but she's still critical. She lost a lot of blood and her ribs are badly bruised. We'll know more in a few hours."

"Can I see her?"

"Not yet. I'll let you know."

I sat on a worn couch in the general waiting room and wept.

When I could catch my breath, I called Joe from my cell. It went to voicemail. No chance I could reach him soon.

I called one of the members of Joe's detective squad and asked what had happened to Rosie Jenkins. I was put through to a friend on Joe's team, Detective Norman O'Hare.

"Sorry about your student, Red. All we know so far is that Rosie Jenkins was found in the parking lot of her apartment house early this morning around five o'clock. Two other tenants reported hearing shots and went down to see what was up. When they found Jenkins, they called us. But she was unconscious when we got there. It was still dark at that hour and no one saw anything."

"Did any of your people check out her apartment?"

"Yes. It was in shambles. Furniture knocked over, broken glass. There was certainly a fight. Our guess now is that someone broke in on her. It looks like she fought back but they beat her up. Then she either ran to the parking lot or was taken there by her attacker and shot. But that's all we know now. We're still investigating."

I told O'Hare about Rosie's email message to me the night before.

There was silence on the other end for a moment. "We don't know much about Danica Boerum's past. But we do know those around her are a rough bunch. If your friend's questioning alarmed Boerum in any way, that might explain what happened last night. But Red, shooting a young woman because you didn't like an interview question? I doubt it. That seems pretty extreme to me. I'm checking out other possibilities."

"Can you check Boerum's people out?"

"We can. But there's something else we both have to consider. Before she came to the university, Rosie Jenkins was a juvenile prostitute for two years then was rescued and sent to rehab."

"I know all about that. What's the relevance?"

Norm coughed. "Last night could have been a guy from her past who's pissed off because she left him. May not have had anything to do with Boerum."

Norm's resistance irritated me. "Rosie's been away from that life for six years. The timing would seem to suggest a more recent event, like her interview with Boerum."

"I'll do what I can, Red. But no one saw anything last night and unless Rosie can identify her attacker, we have nothing to go on right now."

"Do you think her attacker might come after her again?"

"I always assume so."

I ended the call and stared at the pale green walls of the hospital waiting room. I tried to put my cell phone back in my handbag, but my hands refused to obey my brain. I ended up just holding it in my lap.

If Rosie had been right about sex traffickers being dangerous, then all of Joe's reassurances were for nothing. People willing to kill a girl for asking the wrong questions would have no trouble eliminating an undercover cop.

Chapter 10

An hour later Nell and Wynan Congers entered the emergency waiting room. Wynan had his arm tightly around his fiancée.

"We stopped by the police station on our way. That's what took us so long to get here," said Nell. Her arms came around me.

Wynan sat down beside me, and when Nell had completed her hugging, he transferred his arm to my shoulders. "The chief told me Norm O'Hare talked to you. They still have no leads, but he's definitely investigating some of the men around Danica Boerum. Pity Joe's away on assignment. I'm sure you could use him here."

"I sure could." For more than one reason.

"Any news on the girl?"

I shook my head.

"I'm going to get us some coffee from the cafeteria," said Nell.

The thin doctor entered the room and stopped short at the sight of the large, muscular black man with his arm around my shoulders.

"Dr. Solaris?"

"This is Wynan Congers. He's a retired police chief who has come to help me. How's Rosie?"

"You can see her for a minute or two, but only that. She's conscious but still critical."

I left Wynan in the waiting room and followed the doctor to an elevator that took us to the third floor. Then she proceeded down the hall and through doors marked "No Admittance." Rosie's room was at the far end near the back stairs. No good, I thought and pulled my cell phone out of my pocket.

"You can't use that here," said the doctor, pausing before the door and frowning up at me.

"There should be a uniformed policeman stationed outside this room. Whoever tried to kill her may try again."

The doctor looked chagrined. "You're right. Go ahead."

O'Hare picked up on the second ring, said he'd already assigned an officer and wondered where the hell he was.

I entered the darkened room. A single lamp was on a table but the light over Rosie's bed had been dimmed. Rosie was so pale her face almost blended into the pillowcase. A large bruise had formed on her cheekbone and her lip was split. Her breathing was shallow and her voice tremulous. "Hi, Red."

I leaned over her, took her small hand in mine and kissed her forehead. "Oh, Rosie. You terrified me."

Her hand gave mine a slight squeeze. "Do you think I just got punished for being stupid?"

"Who did this?"

"I don't know." She struggled with the effort to talk. "He broke into my apartment and hauled me out of bed and slapped me around."

"Hush, Rosie. This can wait for later."

But Rosie was not to be hushed. "I tried to fight back, but he threw me into a corner and then he started trashing my place."

"A man?"

"A big man. Very big. I'd never seen him before. He wore a ski mask over his face so all I can tell you is that he was white, large and strong." She paused and inhaled. "At one point, I got free and opened the door and ran like hell downstairs into the parking lot. I started screaming but no one came. The man followed me. When he tried to force me into a van, I screamed again. He threw me on the ground and raised his foot to stomp me. I don't remember after that."

"You were shot, Rosie. Twice in the stomach."

She winced. "That's why it hurts so bad. Gut shot is the worst."

The doctor came back into the room with a nurse. She pulled at my sleeve. "You'll have to leave now. Our patient needs more medication and some rest." I squeezed Rosie's hand and walked out with the doctor, who turned to me outside the room. "She's too weak for more conversation now. Come back tomorrow. And please tell your friends in the police that she's not ready to be questioned. I'm having a hard time persuading one of the detectives."

I'd bet I knew which detective. As if my thought had conjured him up, stocky, gray-haired Norm O'Hare loomed into sight, his hand firmly locked on the arm of a lanky boy in a police uniform. Norm directed the officer to grab a chair by the nurses' station and set it against the wall opposite Rosie's room. "Donovan here went to the wrong floor," Norm muttered.

The doctor moved protectively in front of Rosie's door. "She's not ready for you yet, Detective."

I drew Norm aside. "She's very weak, but she did tell me the man who attacked her was a large white man she did not recognize. He wore a ski mask. He pulled her out of her bed, beat her up, trashed her place. She got free of him and ran downstairs into the lot. He followed and tried to shove her into a van. Then he threw her to the ground and she thought he was going to stomp her with his foot. That's all she could tell me."

"The longer we wait for a description of the man and the van..."

"I know, but she's a good reporter. She'll tell you everything she saw as soon as she's a little stronger." I looked at the round face of Officer Donovan now standing at rigid attention by the chair. "By the way, your officer looks like he's still in high school. Will he know what to do if that guy comes back for her?"

"New recruit. First time guarding a patient in the hospital. But he's strong and a good shot."

I gave a long look at Officer Donovan. He'd better be, I thought.

"I'd feel better with someone more experienced manning that post."

Norm gave me a condescending smirk. "Joe told me you held strong opinions, Dr. Solaris. But he didn't tell me you would instruct me on how to do my job."

"Sorry, Norm. But that girl means a great deal to me."

"I understand. We'll watch her very carefully."

Norm turned and walked down to the end of the hall to check the door to the stairwell and for any windows large enough to admit a man. He came back slowly, scanning the walls and the ceiling.

He scratched his chin and stopped at the door to Rosie's room. "Any word from Joe?"

That surprised me. I would have expected Joe to stay more in touch with Norm than with me just to be sure that Landry cases were being handled in his absence. I frowned. Norm looked uncomfortable but cleared his throat and faced me. I took a deep breath.

"As a matter of fact, I haven't heard from Joe for a few days now and it worries me."

"Hmm."

Boy, did I not like that "hmm."

*   *   *

Back in my office, my first call was to the chief of the Landry Police. His voice was kind and level. Just like Joe's when he was dealing with a difficult subject. "Please don't worry, Dr. Solaris. Joe is a skilled detective and he's had significant undercover experience."

"It's just that I haven't heard from him recently, and he said he would try to call every night. Also, I know he'll want to hear about what happened to Rosie Jenkins."

"I'm sure we'll hear from him soon, and if you like, I'll call the chief in Reno and see what I can find out."

"Thank you. I would appreciate that."

I turned from my desk to the window overlooking the quad. Late afternoon sunlight bounced off grass as green as Ireland. Crocus bloomed under the massive trees that lined the quad. New life. I put my hand over my stomach. Nothing yet to indicate I was carrying it. Had I wanted this child to happen? Had I been deliberately forgetful about taking a pill? If I had, Joe would figure that out. "I'm a detective," he would always say when he was able to remember something I had forgotten or discover something I had overlooked.

Would he wonder if I had gotten pregnant so he would propose? Nonsense. I'd never even hinted at marriage. I wasn't sure I wanted to be married. How did I feel now? Would I want this child if I were with any other man? Could I answer that one? The idea of a child of my own thrilled me, but raising one on my own? Or raising a child fathered by a man I didn't love deeply? No thanks.

On the other hand, raising a child of Joe Morgan's? You bet.

* * *

An hour later, the chief called me back. "Sorry I don't have better news. Joe left his job at the casino two days ago. The team Reno PD had keeping an eye on him are looking for him now. They'll call me when they find him. Meanwhile, don't get too worried about him. Joe's the smartest cop I've ever known. I'm sure he's fine."

I put down the phone and glanced up at the door to my office. Phyllis Baker was leaning against the doorframe. "Got a minute?"

"Come in, please. For you, I have more than a minute."

She walked in slowly. Phyllis was slender enough to sit in one of the small chairs in front of my desk. No smile, but a warm look in her eyes. "I hear you gave the Faculty Senate a rasher about freedom of speech."

"Who told you that?"

"Thea Gray and I are pals. She said you were very impressive."

"I'm glad she thought so."

Phyllis smoothed the navy-blue wool skirt over her long legs. Her fingers lingered on the fabric. A long pause preceded her question. "Are you really planning to go to that Purist thing?"

"I know I should after shooting my mouth off and to show some support for my own beliefs. But I don't want to. The thought of sitting through her racist bullshit makes my stomach ache."

Phyllis nodded her head and looked sympathetic. I told her about what had happened to Rosie Jenkins.

"Christ almighty. Those people are not just racists, they may be every bit as dangerous as I suspected."

"We're not sure the man who attacked Rosie works for

Boerum. It's just that the timing of the attack, right after her telephone interview, makes us suspicious."

Phyllis stared at her hands in her lap. "I don't want anything bad to happen to you."

"I don't either."

Phyllis stood up. "Give Rosie my best when you see her. That kid's a good writer even if she takes dumb risks with her interviews."

"Thanks for stopping by. It helps to know we're still friends."

"Always, Red. Always."

Chapter 11

Three more days passed and no call from Joe. Landry PD were no wiser. The chief kept trying to reassure me, but my anxiety went undiminished. Morning sickness attacked with a vengeance. My temper rose, and I wept spontaneously at little setbacks. Rosie was healing, but her condition was still serious and she was still in danger, twenty-four hour police protection notwithstanding.

Nell made extra cups of strong tea and walked through her duties with a furrowed brow. At home, Charlie mimicked her, following me around the house like a service dog attending a patient given to seizures. Two nights in a row, Sadie came over with dinner she had made to keep me company and to make sure I was eating "nourishing and organically grown food."

But I was beside myself. Something had gone wrong with Joe's assignment. He had never let this much time go by without calling. I knew I was being a nervous "cop's woman" about it, but I was frightened for him. And for me without him.

On the third day, I decided to do more research on sex traffickers. I went to see the psychologist who had helped Rosie rehabilitate and introduced us on the first day of her freshman year. Dr. Sonia Ortiz welcomed me into her office in a small, elegantly decorated house at the edge of Landry. I filled her in on the story of Joe's search for Rosie's cousin and the attack on

Rosie. Sonia was a professional consultant to the police as well as a good friend, and I knew I could trust her to keep my confidence.

Sonia's normally calm face paled when I described the attack on Rosie. "Jesus, that's terrible. Will Rosie be all right?"

"She'll recover but it will take a while. Mostly I'm very worried about Joe."

Sonia got up from her chair and walked to the window. After a long moment she spoke.

"As a psychologist I shouldn't scare you, but as your friend I have to be honest with you. You should be worried about him, Red. Sex traffickers are often drug dealers or former drug dealers. You've read about the massacres in Mexico and Central America. These guys mutilate and kill anyone who betrays them or gets in their way. They don't hesitate and they often leave the bodies in a public place as a warning to others."

The expression on my face must have alarmed her.

"I'm sorry," she said.

"But these guys are Americans. Pimps not killers." I heard the note of desperation in my voice.

"If they deal in stolen children and drugs, they're dangerous. I've helped prepare girls to testify against bastards like the one who attacked Rosie. I wish I could be more comforting to you."

"I have to help in some way. I asked Joe to find Rosie's cousin, and now I'm going crazy sitting home and worrying about him."

"Be careful, Red. I know you are good at being an amateur detective, but these guys don't mess around. They're not just deadly, they're smart. They use burner phones to communicate and they mask their websites and change locations often. Even with good technology, the police have a tough time tracking them much less arresting them. Going undercover to get hard evidence is probably the most effective way. Trust Joe to know how."

"When I think something bad might happen to Joe, I can hardly think at all." I rose to leave.

Sonia walked me to the door with her arm around my shoulder. "Try to think good thoughts and give my very best to Rosie. I'll visit her in the hospital. She's one of my success stories."

I was grateful to Sonia for her candor, but I knew I still had to do something. I drove home and called Wynan. "I need your help."

Wynan was sitting at my kitchen table fifteen minutes later. His face gave no readable expression as he listened to my ranting. His voice was calm.

"If Joe's in deep undercover, he may not be able to call you. He may have connected with the group he was targeting. They may have taken away his cell phone while they check him out. Pimps are paranoid about anyone new in their neighborhood. They see cops everywhere."

"I know this." I was fighting back tears. "I just have this unshakable feeling something has happened and Joe's in trouble, trouble he can't get out of."

Wynan took my hand. "You know you're projecting what happened to Rosie onto what might happen to Joe. Let's do this. Rather than have me bug the local chief, how about you and I go to Reno tomorrow and talk to the chief there. Police don't send someone undercover without setting up some contact for the undercover agent to use in an emergency."

Wynan's large hand over mine was gentle and reassuring. "Okay," I said, stifling a sob. "Will the Reno chief tell me anything? I'm not Joe's wife, and even if I were…"

"The Reno chief will tell me anything I need to know. We served together in Vegas years ago. We're friends."

*   *   *

Somehow I made it through another day at school, answering phone calls and letters, reassuring the faculty who taught Rosie that she was, indeed, getting better, reassuring the student newspaper staff that their leader would be back with them soon, and meanwhile, they probably should sit on the story of her attack until the police had a chance to discover more.

I stayed in for lunch prepared by Nell. Tea and a sandwich. All I could think about was waiting for Wynan to call and tell me when we could see the Reno chief.

At one point, Nell came in holding an exam I had written for my ethics students. "You put the wrong date on this," she said gently. "Would you like me to proofread it before I make copies?"

"I guess so," I said with a weakness in my voice I had not heard for a long time. I feared I was losing it. Then the phone rang and, mercifully, Wynan said he had worked things out.

The drive from Landry to Reno took about an hour in light traffic. Once inside the city limits, it was easy to forget you were in high desert country.

In the older residential areas, houses with manicured lawns and big trees lined the streets. Flowering shrubs bloomed near the sidewalks; lilacs were budding and yellow Forsythia was browning up and already saying goodbye. A glimpse of one shaded backyard and front lawn could fool you into thinking you were in New Jersey.

Downtown was different: tall office buildings and neon-covered casino hotels. The new headquarters of the police station were in a commercial section located near City Hall and the main library.

The chief was cordial and glad to see Wynan. He stood at least six foot eight and made my impressive companion seem short in comparison. He welcomed us into a neat but not exceptionally large office and sat us at a conference table. Soft drinks and water sat on a tray.

The chief had a rugged face lined with deep furrows in tan skin. He sat behind his desk and came right to the point. "I'm sorry I don't have specific news I can give you to make you feel better, Dr. Solaris. But, as I'm sure Wynan has explained, when a detective goes undercover, we are often as much in the dark as anyone until he or she makes contact."

"Does Joe have a specific person to contact?"

"He does. He also has a team that keeps an eye on him when possible." The chief and Wynan exchanged looks. "But it's not always possible, and sometimes when someone is undercover we just have to wait for them to find an opportunity to call. As I'm sure you know, what Detective Morgan is doing is very risky, and he has to be extremely careful to maintain his cover."

"When was the last time the contact heard from him?" The chief fixed me with a softened expression.

Wynan put his hand on my shoulder.

The chief coughed. "About a week ago, Morgan met with the contact. They spoke for maybe two minutes. Morgan said he had connected with a group of traffickers and thought he was in with them and trusted enough to be given the job of driving one of their vans between here and Sacramento." The chief gave another look in Wynan's direction. "We think he's on the road most of the time but still being watched. So he has to be careful."

"I thought he was supposed to pose as a pimp from Chicago looking to buy back one of his girls."

"He did. And that's his cover. But when the opportunity to learn about the routes and schedules for bringing girls in and out of Reno came up, he took it. He's hoping...we're all hoping to make a number of arrests soon."

"Who is his contact?"

"Sorry, I can't tell you that."

I sat back in my chair, exhausted and filled with anger and frustration.

"Red, why don't you wait for me in the car? The chief and I have some catching up to do."

It was clear I was not going to learn any more, and the look on Wynan's face suggested he might be able to get useful information out of his old friend if I left them alone in the room. I stood up, thanked the chief and headed for the door, eager to get some air and a chance to think by myself. "I'm going to walk over to the library, Wynan. Please come find me there."

The air outside had turned cooler and the sky overhead was gray. A light spring rain had started to fall, and in the high desert, rain was good news.

I pulled up the hood of my coat and started to walk toward the library. It was one of my favorite places in Reno. A good place to think quietly and sort out my increasing anxiety. The Reno library was a block away and the architecture alone enchanted me. A massive atrium filled with plants invited even those not in search of a book, just perhaps a tranquil moment away from the city's bustle.

I noticed a man crossing the street, his face hidden behind an umbrella. He wore a shabby tweed overcoat, too heavy for the warm spring weather. Something about his stride made my neck tingle.

I increased my pace toward the library. The man reached my side of the street and lifted the umbrella. I almost fainted.

"Hello, Meredith."

I looked into the face of a man who had once terrified me, who had once been my worst enemy. He was more wrinkled now and stooped with age, but still fierce looking and armed with an umbrella and a sturdy cane at his right side. I had to catch my breath and decide whether to run back into the police building or speak.

"Hello, Simon."

Simon Gorshak stepped closer and tucked the cane under his left elbow. He hesitated a moment and then held out his hand. I was dumbfounded. This was the man who had tried to destroy me and all my hopes for a career as a dean. "You look well, Dean Solaris."

My hand stayed at my side. "What are you doing here?"

"I live near here now."

I nodded. My breathing was shallow and the instinct to run was powerful.

"Please don't be alarmed, Meredith. I'm quite changed from the person I was before."

I stared at him. Changed? Not likely. Simon had been the kind of enemy one never forgets or forgives. At one point, when he was still on the journalism faculty, I was convinced he had killed the former dean and was set on killing me. I had been wrong, but he still frightened the living daylights out of me.

"It's good to hear you say you've changed, Simon. You were dreadful before." After I was appointed interim dean, Simon was furious and had threatened me at every opportunity.

His chin went down and he sighed. "I know I was dreadful. And I know I owe you a profound apology."

I was still stunned. And unconvinced.

He looked up, his pale eyes no longer filled with hatred. Now he was just a tired old man. "Meredith, if you could just give me a few minutes. There's something I need to tell you, a confession of sorts. I need to make amends for my sins against you. I would very much like to buy you a coffee."

"Coffee?"

"Yes. There's a small coffee shop back there just across the street if you would be so kind."

I'll never really know why I agreed to sit down with Simon Gorshak, but something in his eyes tugged at me. Besides, the coffee shop was right across from police headquarters and I decided I could leave anytime. Instinct overwhelmed logic, yet it turned out to be the best decision I made during that entire afternoon in Reno.

The shop was small. The furniture seemed new and the paint looked fresh. Two patrolmen sat at the counter. I figured Simon would not do anything dangerous this close to the police. Bright leather-covered chairs and wooden tables sat in a row before a long bar with wooden stools. Other than the two patrolmen, we were the only patrons. I sat us by the front window so I could keep a lookout for Wynan when he left headquarters.

A pretty waitress, resplendent in clanging bracelets and extra earrings, took our orders and came back with coffee for him. Simon twisted the fingers on his bony hands and remained silent until she had left us.

I reconsidered. I would get up and walk out. Simon had called me some disgusting names, insulted my professionalism and made my first days as interim dean absolutely miserable.

His eyes pleaded and I seemed stuck to my seat.

"I was in terrible shape when I was at the university," Simon began. "My wife's decision to leave me and then her death made me lose my mind. I was obsessed with the thought that my only salvation was to become dean again after Henry's death. I despised you and all the others who supported you."

"You behaved dreadfully." I remained cold and remote, waiting for Simon to turn into his old snarling self and lash out at me. But I was no longer afraid of him. Even in my confusion, I knew I could handle whatever was going to happen next.

His bony hand seemed barely able to lift his cup. "I did behave dreadfully. And now I regret all the damage I did to the school and all the damage I tried to do to you."

The sky darkened. Heavier rain hit the sidewalk. "You said you had a confession."

He took a sip from his cup. "The notes that were in your mailbox."

Oh God, those terrifying notes telling me to go back to Ohio or I would meet the same fate that sent Henry to his death.

"I always thought you must be the person who wrote them."

"I was."

The rain increased and the wind came up and blew drops onto the window. Simon and I sat in silence. I thought about the terror I'd felt when I read those notes. Joe and I had both been certain my life was in peril.

I could barely look at Simon, but finally I found my words. "Why did you write anonymous notes? I remember you had no trouble insulting me to my face."

"I didn't write the notes to insult you. I wrote them to frighten you."

"Well, you did, damn you." I braced my hands against the table edge. It was time to leave.

"Meredith, please don't go."

"What more do you have to say?"

"That I was terribly wrong. I've kept tabs on the school since I left. I know now that you were the right person to be dean and that you've done a wonderful job."

I stared at him. Wrinkles lined his gray eyes and ran down his cheeks. An attempt at a sad smile played around his thin mouth. "Please forgive me."

I relaxed and breathed deeply. "You gave me a fearful shock, Simon. I was sure you intended to kill me. Joe said he received a report you'd bought a gun."

"I did, but not to harm you or anyone at the school. It was just for protection. I live in a dangerous neighborhood here and I'm old. I walk home through a street of pimps and whores and even the women frighten me now."

Pimps and whores. The people Joe was seeking. I wondered if Simon had seen him. But I was still wary. I had to be cautious.

"Do you see anyone from Landry?"

"No. But I'd like to see Edwin again, and maybe one or two others about a book I'm writing. Do you think Edwin would meet with me?" Edwin Cartwell had once been Simon's ally but had turned against him when Simon tried to damage the school.

I looked long and hard at Simon Gorshak. Now, all I saw was a fragile old man, alone and in need. It was hard to keep seeing him as a threat to me or anyone. "I'll ask Edwin. Give me your number and address, and I'll let him decide if he wants to contact you."

Simon reached into his coat pocket and pulled out a small stack of cards. He peeled one off the top, and his hand trembled as he gave it to me. It was plain, just his name, address and telephone number. The corners were bent and the stock was dirty. I suspected those cards had spent a long time in his pocket, unused and unneeded.

We both stood. "Thank you. And thank you for your time today."

"It was a relief to find out you never meant to kill me," I said, trying to smile. "Good luck with the book."

"You're a kind woman, Meredith Solaris. Kinder than I deserve."

I shook his cold hand and headed for the door. I could see Wynan emerging from the police station as I went out into the rain.

*   *   *

The swish of the wipers on Wynan's windshield was the only sound in the car as we drove back through the streets of Reno to the freeway.

"You're very quiet," he said as we came to the ramp leading up to the route that would take us home.

"I ran into someone I hadn't seen for a long time. An old enemy who turned out not to be a danger to me after all. Joe will be happy to hear about this when I see him again."

"I'm afraid it may be a while before either of us sees Joe." Wynan's voice was low and soft. His eyes fixed on the road and his hands gripped the steering wheel. My stomach muscles contracted.

"You found out something else from the chief."

"I found out about Joe's contact." Wynan cleared his throat and slowed a bit. The rain was coming down in sheets and the road was slick.

"Something the chief didn't want me to know, right?"

"Right. And you'll have to keep this to yourself. Police don't like civilians being informed about their business."

"Wynan, for God's sake, tell me..."

Wynan inhaled and kept his eyes straight ahead on the dark road. "Seems Joe's contact was another undercover cop working as a bartender in the casino where Joe was a pit boss before he joined the trafficking ring."

"And?"

Rain pelted the window, obscuring the view ahead.

"The bartender got into a fight two days ago in an alley behind the casino. He's now in the hospital with stab wounds, a severe concussion and a broken jaw." Wynan, eyes fixed on the road, inclined his head toward me and his big hand came over mine for a moment. "Sorry, Red. This is not good. It means Joe probably can't get to his contact but still has to maintain his cover."

The pit of my stomach turned to ice. "Joe's out there on his own."

"The Reno PD are looking for him, but..."

"He's alone."

I lay in bed that night and let the tears I'd held in all afternoon finally come. They streamed down the side of my face and dampened the pillowcase. Joe Morgan had disappeared and might be dead. Wynan said he refused to believe Joe was dead, but if Joe's contact had been beaten and stabbed, what did that mean? Alone in the dark, I imagined the worst: Joe's unconscious body crumpled up in a car trunk. Then I saw him on his knees in the desert with a gun pointing to the back of his head. In Nevada there were still bodies buried in the desert that had never been found.

Joe's beautiful body. Long, lean muscles, tender hands, thick dark hair, wonderful green eyes. My Joe, who read poetry and watched basketball with equal passion. The one man I had ever really wanted to share my life with. If the baby was a boy, please let him look like his father.

I felt a thump as my dog landed on the bed and put his soft nose into my neck.

"Oh, Charlie. You haven't been allowed in this bed since the night Joe named you." I put my hand around his silky body and pulled him close. "Remember? I couldn't come up with a good name for you and Joe named you Charlie. And later Joe told me Charlie had been the name of his best friend. And Charlie had died his senior year in..." My sobbing took the words away from me, and I lay in my damp bed holding my dog and trying with all my might to believe in the efficacy of prayer.

Chapter 12

The rain continued through the night and into the next day. The newscaster on the television chirped out the stats in a tone too optimistic to bear. Rain may be good news in the high desert, but I was of no mind to celebrate.

Once settled behind my desk and faced with a pile of folders and a schedule, I resolved to get through as much work as possible in the morning and then get together with Wynan in the late afternoon to plan our next course of action—whatever that would be.

I called Rosie in the hospital. Her voice was getting stronger. Naturally, her first question was about Joe's progress finding Cathy.

"Joe's pretty deep undercover now. So we haven't heard anything from him."

"Oh."

I could hear her disappointment, but it could hardly match the despair I was feeling. "You just concentrate on getting well and helping Norm O'Hare find the guy who did this to you."

"I met with Norm yesterday and told him everything I could remember about the man. I may have given him some helpful information, but we're not sure it will make a difference."

"I'm glad you and Norm talked, Rosie. I'll try to visit you soon."

*   *   *

I walked across campus, hoping it would help me regain my self-confidence and my equilibrium. Daffodils lined the quad. Usually, their bright bobbing heads had a sanguine effect on my disposition. I needed a lift because a plan was beginning to form in my mind, and I knew depression was the antithesis of good strategic thinking.

Maybe there was a way Wynan and I could search for Joe. I fingered the card still in my jacket pocket. Simon had said he owed me. We could start with him. Maybe there was a way he could help us figure a way through the neighborhood of pimps and whores he occupied.

Sadie was reading at her table in Gormley's. "How are you feeling?"

"Mornings are still rough, but your saltine and soda recommendations have helped."

Sadie removed her glasses and stood up to kiss my cheek. I appreciated her unusual gesture. Public affection was not her thing. "The nausea will ease up after a while. Any news of Joe?"

I collapsed in the chair opposite her and began the odyssey of my trip to Reno with Wynan and my encounter with Simon.

"Wow, you had quite a day."

"And quite a night too. I don't think I slept more than an hour or so."

Wilson, who had been standing near enough to hear, poured fresh cups of tea. "Joe Morgan's a big, strong guy who knows how to take care of himself," he said, sitting beside Sadie.

"Didn't know you even liked cops," I said.

Wilson shrugged. "As a rule, I don't. But Joe's the exception. He's a brilliant man. He'll know how to maintain his cover." His expression was uncommonly sympathetic. This was the new Wilson, I had to remind myself.

I was still getting used to the idea of Sadie and Wilson as a couple. Sadie's white hair was thicker than his, but they were of similar height and thinness and both wore the same eyeglasses, which made them look more like siblings than lovers.

I remembered my manners and decided not to prattle on about my anxieties over Joe. "How are you two doing?"

Sadie put her hand over Wilson's. "Better than we expected. We told my son and his wife about our situation last night at dinner."

"How did they take it?"

"My son wished us much happiness. He got up from the table, gave me a hug and kiss, shook Wilson's hand and asked him to take good care of me. It played out just as my son's meeting with his future father-in-law had done ten years ago. So similar, it made his wife laugh."

"How did she react?"

"She kissed Wilson on the cheek and told us she was delighted for us."

Wilson winked. "I felt much like a college boy basking in his in-laws' approval. Curious how things reverse later in life. Both of them were very parental. So, guess what? We're thinking of replacing you and Joe as the new hot couple on the Mountain West campus."

I felt an acute pang of jealousy. I knew I should have been happy for them, but all I could think about was my own distress. They sensed it.

"You going to be all right?" Sadie asked.

"I'm thinking Wynan and I should go look for Joe. Ask Simon to help us, maybe introduce us to someone in that part of Reno who knows where the sex trade flourishes."

Sadie drew back in her chair, appalled. "You're pregnant. You're not thinking straight. Probably lack of sleep. Darling, you can't run around some sort of red light district in Reno looking for an undercover detective. It's stupid and dangerous, for you and for him."

Wilson looked more sympathetic. "We know how much you want to help Joe. But this could backfire, Red. You could get him killed. You could get yourself killed meddling in his work and messing with these people."

"I know. Wynan probably won't agree to it anyway."

"Wynan certainly won't."

But Wynan did agree to listen. He and Nell both showed up at the house ten minutes after I had arrived home. I was feeding Charlie and they were seated at the kitchen table.

Wynan coughed vigorously to clear his throat. "Nell has been telling me about this Simon Gorshak. I don't like the idea of you contacting a man who once threatened your life."

"If I hadn't seen him myself, I wouldn't trust him either." I looked at Nell, who was frowning. "But I honestly think he has changed and his remorse is genuine."

Nell folded her hands on the table, pressing her palms tightly together. Her disapproval was palpable. "He's a hateful man, Red. Have you forgotten he tried to destroy you and the reputation of the school? He didn't just leave those notes in your mailbox, he wrote a letter denouncing the entire school and sent it to all the journalism deans in the country."

"I haven't forgotten anything about him, Nell. And he still gives me the creeps. But he lives in the area where I think Joe's targets live, and he may know something or someone…"

Wynan interrupted, "Let's meet him for coffee. You and me. I'll scope him out and see what I think."

"Wynan, you're terrific. Thank you."

Nell's face was full of protest. "Oh, Wynan. Simon's a terrible man, the devil incarnate."

Wynan took his fiancée's hand and held it tightly. "I can deal with the devil when he has useful information." He looked at me. "Any cold beer in this house tonight?"

I slept better that night even with Charlie's warm fur pressed against me. Charlie in bed was absolutely against the rules according to Joe. Joe would say, "Now I have to retrain him," when he came home and found out.

But until Joe came home, and until I knew he was still alive and able to come home, I chose to break the rules. All of them, if necessary. Contacting Simon again would be strictly against the rules under normal circumstances. So would going into a bad neighborhood. So would asking Wynan to help me with a mission that could be dangerous. All against the rules of common sense.

But I was damned if I was going to go about my regular routines and wait. The man's child grew within me. Of course, that was also against the rules, but what the hell.

I sat in my office for most of the morning before I worked up the courage to call the number on the little card Simon had given me. He answered on the second ring. "I have to say I'm amazed to hear from you. I figured I'd never see you again."

"Simon, I haven't had a chance to talk to Edwin yet, but I do have a favor to ask of you. I'd like to see you again for coffee and bring along a policeman friend of mine."

"Not that Morgan fellow, please. He was very rough on me."

"No, not Joe. Another policeman. I need help with something."

"Well, I do owe you a favor. But I'm tied up with doctor's appointments today."

We agreed to meet the next morning at the same coffee shop.

My head was spinning. The prospect of seeing Simon again made me dizzy and my stomach didn't much like the thought either. I needed some fresh air and once again decided to walk outside in hopes of clearing my head.

"You leaving us again?" asked Nell as I marched to the outer office door. I felt a twinge of guilt. I had spent a lot of time out of the office and still hadn't told Nell I was pregnant.

"Fresh air for a few minutes," I replied. "Run the school for me."

"I can, you know," she said with a raised eyebrow.

The grass on the quad had just been mowed. Probably my favorite scent, but not that day. I had to plan carefully for the meeting with Simon. An idea was forming in my mind about how to help Joe, and I needed clarity. The concrete walks behind the College of Science did nicely. Rows of neatly trimmed and odorless boxwood punctuated the paths.

About five minutes into the walk I slowed down and began to notice the posters pinned to streetlamps and kiosks. "Danica Boerum," they announced in three-inch high letters. A large photo of her face separated her name from bulleted text below: "We are a Christian Country" and "Send non-Europeans home."

I didn't bother to read more. As I passed the third poster, I spotted a Hitler-like mustache drawn on her face and the words "Nazi Bigot Bitch" scrawled over the text.

Still a few days left before her appearance and already the ugliness was manifesting. I tucked away my plan and kept on walking. I knew the former fraternity house that the student Purists had purchased was another hundred yards down the path, and I decided to pay a visit.

A banner announcing Boerum's speech ran across the full width of the upper balcony, concealing the elegant lines of the three-story white house. It had been one of the first buildings on campus and home to three successive university presidents in the early part of the twentieth century before being sold to a fraternity who let it run down and then sold it again.

The Purists had cleaned it up. Fresh paint on the front steps and new dark green shutters on the tall first-floor windows. Primroses planted in huge pots flanked the large mahogany front door. This was not just for Danica Boerum. The house had been pristine ever since the Purists took it over. Whatever one might say of them, the Purists were a tidy group. Maybe I could persuade them to take down the offensive posters, limit the publicity and the size of the crowd.

A slender boy with a face as smooth as porcelain opened the door. He was dressed formally for a student: white shirt, dark striped tie, navy trousers. Elegant shoes, expensive oxfords, not sneakers. "Can I help you?"

"I was wondering if the president of your group was in."

"He's still in class. But our vice president is here. Would you like to speak to her?"

"Thank you. I would."

The boy ushered me into a front hall dominated by a massive staircase carpeted in red, the bannister dark and shining. He led me down the hall into a sitting room at the end. The furnishings were traditional and immaculate, two leather sofas and four wing chairs upholstered in dark green velvet.

The boy indicated a chair and then stood in front of me, one pale white hand folded neatly across his abdomen, the other behind his back in the pose of an English butler. Very *Downton Abbey*. "Would you like something to drink, ma'am? Coffee or water?"

"Water would be great, thank you."

He disappeared. I sat in one of the chairs and ran my hands over the thick fabric. Horsehair velvet. Very expensive. Hardly typical for a student living room.

"Nice to see you, Dr. Solaris." A tall girl with perfectly

highlighted long beige hair walked toward me, a glass of water in her hand.

"I'm sorry. Do I know you?"

"I was enrolled in your ethics class two years ago, but I left after two sessions." She handed me the water glass and sat perched on the arm of one of the sofas, her pleated dark skirt fanning nicely around long slim legs. "I'm Alexandra Pickering."

And I'll bet a month's salary you don't tolerate a nickname. I sipped the cool water. "Nice to see you again, Alexandra. You're the vice president of the Purists?"

"There are three VPs. I'm VP of events."

"So you're in charge of Danica Boerum's appearance here?"

She paused for a sweet smile and a fluttering of eyelashes. "I am. Are you here to lecture me about that?"

"No. I'm here to ask you about all the posters on campus. And I heard a radio commercial driving to work this morning. Why all the advertising? I thought her appearance was a private event for your group alone."

Another eyelash flutter. "Not really. We rather hope some others from the community will want to hear what Leader Boerum has to say."

"I see. Don't you think that so much publicity might draw trouble to your event?"

"More water, Dr. Solaris?"

I shook my head.

She rose and walked to the window, tossing her hair so it caught the sunlight, a move so deliberate I was sure she practiced it.

"We are used to trouble, Dr. Solaris. Just as we are used to being misunderstood." She turned back to me. "But we are not deterred by trouble. We welcome it. Trouble attracts sympathizers to our mission and our mission is essential."

"Your mission?"

A dazzling smile. "To restore our country to the greatness it enjoyed in 1776."

I nearly choked, but regained my control. "Our country was a collection of struggling colonies in 1776. Our original leaders fought each other almost as ferociously as they had fought the British."

Alexandra turned back to the window.

I pressed on, "We didn't get together as a nation until some years later, and the Constitution wasn't written until 1787. Is that the kind of struggle and uncertainty you want us to go back to?"

Smugness replaced cordiality. The smile turned to the pouty lower lip and defiant eyes I had learned to associate with twenty-year-olds who are certain they know everything.

"I think you understand what I'm saying, Dr. Solaris."

I stood up and turned for the door. "Oh, I understand what you're saying, Alexandra. Although given your curious reading of American history, I am not altogether sure *you* understand what you're saying."

Chapter 13

My walk back to the journalism school was speedier. My head was not much clearer but my resolve was stronger. Alexandra had tipped her hand, although I'm sure she wouldn't have seen it that way.

I called the provost. "Manny, have you met with the student leaders yet about this Boerum speech?"

"A small group. I plan to meet with a larger group later this week."

"May I join you for that meeting?"

"Love to have you. What's on your mind?"

"I'll put it in an email tonight, but I have some thoughts on how we might help our students keep the peace."

"You expect new kinds of trouble?"

"Not new trouble, but I now have a feeling the Purists welcome discord and violence. I suspect they believe it helps disseminate their ideology."

"Well, it certainly gains them publicity."

"I think they want more than publicity. I think maybe they want martyrdom."

"Shit. So they're setting us up. I'll look for your email."

Later that afternoon, I drove to the hospital. I knew I should see Rosie again, and I wanted to make sure her room was still well guarded and safe for her. She was awake, propped against pillows eating soup. A touch of color in her cheeks made her look much healthier.

"Hi, Red."

"You look one hundred percent better than my last visit. Is the food really that good?"

"The food's moderately acceptable, what I can eat of it, but hardly good."

I sat on the edge of her bed. "And how's the stomach?"

"Still painful but not agonizing. My spleen was nicked but the docs say no other vital organs were injured."

"But they're watching the spleen for bleeding?"

"Yup. They watch me all the time. So do the cops assigned to guard me. Last night's Officer Donovan was kind of cute."

"Remind me to tell you someday about the pitfalls of flirting with good-looking cops. But more important, have you and Norm made any headway on identifying your attacker?"

Rosie shifted in bed, wincing slightly. "I've wracked my brain trying to describe the man. I know he was white because I saw his hands. I know he was tall and very strong, but he said practically nothing so I still have no idea what he came for, except to hurt me or kill me."

"Well, as long as he doesn't show up here."

"If he does, I have an army of uniforms hanging around. In fact, here's one now. Good evening, Officer Donovan."

I turned to see the youthful cop Norm had brought over right after Rosie's surgery. Donovan's expression betrayed a special interest in Rosie. He actually blushed at her greeting.

I got up to leave.

"Come back tomorrow night," said Rosie. "Danica Boerum's going to be interviewed on Las Vegas television. They're going to re-run it here. We can scope her out together."

"I'm going to be in Reno part of the day, but I'll do my best to get back here."

"Red?"

"What?"

"Thanks for being such a good mom. These last few days I've needed one."

I must have still been smiling at Rosie's remark when Helen Ferguson and I met in the hospital corridor, because she greeted me with an uncharacteristic grin of her own. "You look a good deal happier than you were in my office the other day."

"I'm starting to get used to the idea of motherhood."

"Have you told your guy yet?"

"Not yet. He's still out of town, and I want to tell him in person."

Helen planted her feet in front of me. Her eyes were full of merriment. "Well, when you do tell him, you can also prepare him for a due date the last week of October or, if you're late, early November. The tests came back and you are in superb health and should ready yourself for a complex holiday season."

Late fall. What was happening in late fall? Nell's wedding, but that would be here in Landry. Any important foreign conferences? Any airplane trips I had already scheduled to take and would now have to cancel? What difference did it make? Sometime between Halloween and Thanksgiving, I was going to have a baby. Wow. What else could possibly matter?

The next morning, Wynan arrived at my house promptly at nine and settled into a kitchen chair as if he had lived in my house all his life. That made me feel good, since Wynan had been very formal and ill at ease with me when we first met.

"I've done a little checking on your Simon Gorshak since we last spoke," he said, sipping his cup of coffee. We were due to meet Simon at ten.

"He's not *my* Simon."

"In any event, he seems to have kept his nose clean since leaving here. He does have a gun permit, but so far he's never used the gun that we know of."

"He claims it's for protection because he lives in a bad neighborhood."

"Well, he does live in an area where there are gangs and a number of seedy motels. But that may be because he doesn't have much money. The background check I did tells me he doesn't seem to have income other than Social Security and whatever he gets from his pension, so I would guess he needs a cheap apartment."

"Simon forfeited a lot when he left Mountain West. His retirement savings went to care for his alcoholic wife in a hospital. I think there's a high probability he was in deep debt by the time she died."

"Unlucky bastard."

"He was a bastard to me, but maybe he'll take this chance to make amends and help us out."

"Let's go see."

Simon was waiting for us at a table in the back of the coffee shop. In spite of the warming weather, he was wearing a shabby tweed overcoat. He stood when we approached the table and held out his bony hand to me and then to Wynan as I introduced him. He was reserved and polite, displaying none of the savagery of his former days.

We ordered while Wynan sat quietly sizing up Simon. The older man sensed he was being scrutinized.

"I'm not any danger to her, you know."

Wynan nodded. "Not with me around."

Simon turned to me. "You said on the phone that you might need my help. What can I do?"

"Thank you, Simon. I appreciate you taking this time. Deputy Chief Congers and I are looking for a man who's involved in sex trafficking here in Reno. We need a contact, someone who knows the area and the traffickers and would be willing to help us out."

"Regrettably, that would not be me." He sipped his tea and his eyes took on a squint. "I make it a point to avoid such people. Why not call on the Reno police?"

"We've tried them and think we'll do better on our own."

Wynan leaned forward and employed that friendly smile cops sometimes use to get information. "Dr. Gorshak, perhaps you know someone who could provide us a contact."

Simon stared at the table. "Perhaps."

"Please, Simon."

"Never thought I'd hear you say please to me, Meredith. After the way I treated..." His voice thickened.

"This is really important. It involves a child. And for the child's sake, we cannot use police," I said.

Simon's chest heaved. "I do know a woman who might still have someone she knows in that world. She's a former prostitute. No longer in the game, but she lives near me. We have the occasional meal together. Nothing between us, mind you."

"Just a friend."

"Right, just a friend." His voice was steady, but somehow I doubted I was getting the truth about his relationship to his woman friend.

Wynan's look hardened. "Could you give us her name and address?"

"Not just yet." Simon rubbed his thin gray hands together. "I'll have to talk to her first and see if she's willing. She's not too fond of police, but she might be willing to talk to Meredith."

I pulled a card out of my handbag and gave it to Simon.

"Will you try to contact her today and call my cell phone as soon as you know if I might see her?"

He fingered my card gingerly and then looked at me with watery eyes. "I want to help, so I'll do my best. But no guarantees."

Wynan pulled out his notebook. "Mind if I get your address and number?" Simon reached into his pocket and handed Wynan another card like the one he had given me.

"This still your current number and address?" Wynan asked, a flash of fierceness in his eyes.

"I don't dissemble, Chief Congers," said Simon, drawing himself up to look Wynan directly in the eye.

"Let's hope not," said Wynan with pretended cordiality. "Dissemblers don't do well with me."

The three of us left the coffee shop. I stood with Simon while Wynan walked a few yards ahead of us talking on his cell phone.

I held out my hand to Simon. "Thank you, Simon. If you can help us with this, you will be helping to save a life. Maybe two lives."

A pursing of his thin lips as he looked at Wynan, and then he turned away.

I caught up with Wynan as he was finishing his call. "That was Reno PD," he said. "No word from Joe yet, but I checked out Simon's address. I think we might just drive over to that neighborhood and take a look."

We drove for a few blocks and watched the bright cleanliness of downtown Reno gradually turn to a grayer, seedier set of buildings. Simon lived in a neighborhood of motels, vacant lots and rundown houses with chain-link fences barring visitors from ragged lawns full of trash and old cars on blocks. We suspected few people walked the street during the day and even fewer at night. There were no visible stores or supermarkets. Four-story apartment houses occupied two of the corners. One was Simon's. It had been a hotel half a century ago.

Some single-family homes still remained, most of them in need of cleaning and paint. "Room for rent" signs were frequent. The first sign of life came from a line of bedraggled men waiting to get into a homeless shelter that dominated the corner.

"So this is where men come looking for sex?"

"Not here," said Wynan, coming to a sudden stop to allow a slow-moving figure to inch his way in front of the car. "This is just where the girls are housed. The sex happens in motels and hotel rooms back in the better parts of town."

"How do the men find the girls? I don't see any streetwalkers."

"Oh, there are probably some at night on the main drags. But now most of the contact is arranged through the internet. The customer makes his choice online. The girl is delivered to the customer at his room. The trade is much more out of sight."

As if to contradict Wynan, two girls appeared on the other side of the intersection. Each was wearing high boots and very short skirts. One had a yellow wool shawl wrapped around her thin shoulders, the other a sweater stretched across impressive breasts. But they didn't seem to be soliciting, just hurrying to cross the street before the light changed.

"Coming home from a long night," said Wynan, speeding up as soon as the light turned green. We had both had enough of Simon's neighborhood.

Back in Landry, I had to rush to get to my Media Ethics class in time. I hated it when students wandered in after class began, so I tried to set a good example and get there ten minutes early.

The class topic was pertinent: trigger warnings. The subject had been heavily covered in the media and the debate raged in academic journals with headlines such as "Freedom of Speech under Attack." A perfect topic for this week's class.

I had divided the class up in teams, requesting each team take a different perspective. Students would debate the topic in class. One of my brightest was already rehearsing her presentation. The girl brushed her hair back from her face with one hand and waved me over to her as I entered.

"I've got a killer quote here, Red. It was written by Judith Shulevitz in the *New York Times*. Listen: 'People ought to go to college to sharpen their wits and broaden their field of vision. Shield them from unfamiliar ideas, and they'll never learn the discipline of seeing the world as other people see it. They'll be unprepared for the social and intellectual headwinds that will hit them as soon as they step off campuses.'" The girl paused, her face flushed.

"That's good, Abby."

"Wait, there's more, Red. She writes: 'What will they do when they hear opinions they've learned to shrink from? If they want to change the world, how will they learn to persuade people to join them?'"

"I see you're preparing your students to do battle." The voice belonged to Edwin Cartwell, former antagonist, great teacher and, of late, newfound friend. Whenever I felt blue, I'd head for one of Edwin's writing classes. Watching him teach reminded me of how much I love the work we do in a university. Edwin was the sort of teacher students remember all their lives. "This is the man who taught me how to write," said a famous author visiting on campus last year. "That was after he taught me how to think."

Every so often Edwin flatters me by sitting in on one of my classes.

"You joining us today, Dr. Cartwell?"

Edwin had a boyish grin and would have looked younger if his hair was not so thin. "I heard your students are going to debate the merits of requiring professors to issue trigger warnings whenever they plan to discuss something someone might consider controversial."

"It would save many of us from being offended in our own classrooms," said another girl who had come in. She slammed her backpack down on the desk.

"It also might save you from learning how to argue intelligently," said a boy walking in just behind her.

I held up my hands. "Okay, okay, everyone. Let's save it for the discussions in class. You'll all have a chance to express your opinions."

Edwin chuckled. "Oh, I'm glad I decided to come to this one. Sounds as if we're in for a lively hour or so."

And he was right on.

Three notions really bugged me. The first was that college students were so fragile that they needed to be spared from hearing ideas and opinions that might offend their personal sensitivities. Second was the use of someone else's race, religion, sexual orientation or physical appearance as a verbal weapon in a dispute. And third was the difficulty too many people have distinguishing between one and two.

I yearned for the common sense needed to study offensive material without taking it personally.

The lively hour proceeded. The students were wonderful, debating back and forth, employing facts and rational arguments, making me proud of them and a little pleased with myself for assigning them the topic.

It ended with one student insisting that her American Literature class be able to read Mark Twain's *Adventures of Huckleberry Finn* out loud even though Twain used "the nword," and another student arguing that the book could "easily be replaced by a better one." I privately decided there are not that many better books but kept it to myself. It was their match to play, not mine.

As the students gathered up their backpacks and streamed out of the classroom, Edwin came over to me. "Good class, Red. It's refreshing to hear students engage in such lively disagreement over what they are supposed to talk about. And speaking of disagreement, are you planning to go to that Danica Boerum thing?"

"I wish I could figure my way out of it, but I seem to have shot my mouth off so much about freedom of speech, I'll be called a hypocrite if I don't go."

Edwin's eyes softened and his hand came to my shoulder. "My deepest sympathies. I share your views on freedom of speech, but I for one plan to stay home and read some D.H. Lawrence just to mark the occasion. I'm old enough to remember when some of his writing was banned in America."

"Go for it, Edwin. I wish I could escape with you."

He left me back in the real world, and I hastened off to see Rosie.

Chapter 14

The hospital in Landry was small but efficient and brighter and cleaner than I had expected when I first moved to Nevada. I still remembered the dreariness of the major metro emergency wards back in Ohio when I was a newspaper reporter. A friend had once said, "I hate just driving by a big city hospital. Infection floats out through the windows and drifts into your car." I thought about that whenever I had to cover a story that took me to hospitals constructed in the nineteenth century.

Rosie's room was on the third floor of a hospital built in the 1990s. The hallway floor was a shiny vinyl and the walls painted a soft blue. Less rushed than on my earlier visits, I had time to admire the long bulletin boards that displayed the imaginative work of fourth graders who had created pictures that would cheer up the patients. Flowers and birds, balloons and fire trucks accompanied me down to the chair where a solemn older cop sat guarding Rosie's room.

A surprising figure came into view from the other end of the hall: Rosie on her feet, stepping slowly with the help of a walker. A nurse followed behind. We met at the door to her room.

"You're amazing," I said, watching her grimace as she slowly maneuvered her way back to bed and got under the covers.

"Just determined. You come to watch TV with me?"

"I wish I could bring you some treats to eat."

"Not just yet," said the nurse. "Her stomach isn't ready for anything exciting."

I nodded at the nurse. "How's your patient doing?"

"Better than most, and no complaints." The nurse adjusted Rosie's pillow. She was a heavyset woman with a broad face and an old-fashioned braid wound around her head. She patted Rosie's shoulder. "This one puts my other patients to shame. Here she is with gunshot wounds that would make grown men cry and she just soldiers on. Cheerful as all get out."

Rosie flashed an accommodating smile. "Hey, I'm still here. When I was lying in that parking lot I thought it was all over for me."

I pulled the visitor's chair closer to her bed so I could see the television screen. "When's Boerum due on?"

"In about five minutes. I think the local station will broadcast the interview live from Las Vegas where she is this week. The Reno affiliate announced earlier that they're broadcasting it here because of Boerum's coming to Mountain West." Rosie pushed a button on the side of her bed and brought herself up to a sitting position. "How was your trip to Reno?"

I didn't tell her about Joe's disappearance. No point in making her think he or his mission were in jeopardy. "Nothing from Joe, but I had a good conversation with a former colleague who may be helpful. And I drove through the neighborhood in Reno where the pimps house the girls."

Rosie's nose wrinkled. "Lovely, isn't it? I remember two weeks in a house that smelled like a cat's litterbox. I shared a room with two other girls and a bathroom with six. But it was still better than the motel we stayed in before the pimps rented the house. At least we had a kitchen and a backyard where we could barbeque in the summer."

I shook my head. "I'm so glad those times are over for you. I can't imagine..."

Her voice sharpened. "No, you can't. No woman who has never been a whore can imagine what it's like." She aimed the remote at the television set suspended on the wall and we both sat silent listening to the commercials that preceded the interview. The Las Vegas news anchor was a handsome man of about thirty who rattled easily through descriptions of traffic accidents and local crimes before announcing his special interview with Danica Boerum, "the woman who speaks for the American Purists and who will appear in person in Las Vegas tomorrow night and at Mountain West University in Landry later this week."

The scene shifted to a smaller studio. Danica sat in an upholstered chair, her long legs sheathed in black stockings. She wore a gray conservative suit with a white blouse and red silk scarf that showed off her snowy short hair. I estimated her age at somewhere between forty and fifty, though her skin seemed smooth with only a trace of crow's feet around her eyes.

The news anchor's opening questions struck me as lightweight and innocuous given the controversies surrounding his guest. Danica remained poised, her voice gentle and controlled. Finally, her interviewer stopped tossing soft balls. "You've been accused by some of causing riots and violence at your appearances. How do you respond to your critics, Miss Boerum?"

A toss of her head signaled a new harshness in her tone, but she kept her cool demeanor. "I don't personally cause riots. I tell the truth about this country and some members of the audience are unwilling to accept it. Any violence is entirely the responsibility of people who cannot bear to face facts."

A sharp intake of breath from Rosie. "Oh God, Red. Her voice just changed. I know that voice."

I took Rosie's hand. "Are you sure? It seems so unlikely she could be related to the woman you knew in Los Angeles."

"I'm not certain. But she could be the older sister to the bitch I knew."

After the interview, Rosie turned off the set. "Well, that was uninformative. We still don't know any more about Boerum or her motives than we did before."

"Tell me more about the woman in Los Angeles."

Rosie slumped down into her pillows. "Her name was Mama D, and she was terrifying. Long black hair and a scary voice that sounded just like Boerum's at the end of that interview. Mama D ran her girls like a drill sergeant, shouting orders at them even in the street where others could hear. I once saw one of her girls give her some back talk and Mama D punched her. The girl was taller and bigger than she was, but Mama D knocked her down in the gutter and kicked her, again and again. Mama D was wearing heavy leather boots and she kicked like she didn't care if she messed the girl up and put her out of business for a week."

"That doesn't sound at all like the Danica Boerum we just saw."

Rosie frowned. "I grant you their personalities are entirely different. The woman in LA was loud and offensive. The woman we just watched is polite and cool, although, for me, equally offensive. But when I talked to her on the phone, she hung up on me when I asked if she'd ever had a relative in LA. And I got beat up and shot the night after. I could be dead wrong, but I think I alarmed her with my question. I feel in my gut...even my injured gut...that there's some connection between Boerum and the meanest woman pimp I ever knew."

Rosie's speculation absorbed me as I drove home from the hospital, but my mood lightened when a familiar car drove into my driveway ahead of me. Sadie's Jeep.

"Just popped over on the off chance of catching you," she said, emerging from the car with a shopping bag in hand. "I brought you some dinner. I was prepared to leave it on the doorstep if you were out."

"I'm delighted. I could use a lift, and I am very happy to see one of the few friends who knows all my fears and secrets."

Sadie put her free arm around my shoulders as we walked into the kitchen, where she gave me a long hug and then pulled a casserole from the shopping bag.

"Stroganoff," she said. "Not as superlative as the one Joe makes, but reasonable enough for a supper for my best friend."

"Can you join me?"

"For a while, but not for long. Himself and I are going to an early movie."

"So Wilson has achieved 'himself' status, I see."

Sadie seated herself at my kitchen table and leaned forward, chin in her hand and a sweet smile on her face.

"Wilson has achieved the impossible. He has returned me to the helpless romantic I was in my twenties. I am absolutely besotted."

"Sex fiend."

"That too. Speaking of sex, any word from the father of your child?"

I shook my head and poured some dry dog food into Charlie's bowl.

Sadie's smile disappeared. "Sorry about that. How about your new relationship with the dreadful Simon Gorshak? How's that going?"

"Wynan and I met with him this morning. He's agreed to try and help us find a contact if he can persuade a former prostitute he knows to cooperate."

"I still think this is stupidly dangerous work for you. You have a baby to consider."

"But I need to find Joe. I really need to find him."

"I know. I want you to find him too. I miss my weekly fix of poetry. It amazes me how he has a perfect memory for poems, lines from literature, even quotes from critics." Sadie, who was clearly trying to distract me from my misery, talked about the past and reminded me of the many dinners she had shared with Joe and me, and the jokes from Joe and more serious long talks we'd had about books.

I joined her reminiscences. "Joe loves literature. Says he always has. A few weeks ago, I showed him a piece I had written for an academic journal and his comment was: 'Good, but too many commas.'"

"Too many commas?"

"Yep. And then he quoted James Thurber to me, how Thurber hated commas and argued with the editors at *The New Yorker*."

Sadie smiled. "Ah, yes. If I recall, Thurber said that commas were: 'so many upturned office chairs hurled down the wide-open corridor of readability.'"

We both laughed. "That's it."

"I'm still amazed a police detective knows and cares about that stuff." Sadie checked her casserole in the oven. "I share your wish to get him back again."

"That's what I hope will happen with my plan."

Sadie pulled the steaming stroganoff out of the oven, and I poured a glass of red wine for her and water for me.

"When do you go back to Reno?" she asked.

"As soon as Simon calls and sets up a meeting."

She frowned and dished up the food. "It's ironic that Simon Gorshak would be the one you have to count on. You're sure he isn't setting some trap for you? He was as dangerous as a rattlesnake the last time you dealt with him."

Sadie's warning gave me pause, but I knew I had to keep

going with my plan. "I have to believe—or hope—that he's sincere. Getting through to Joe is paramount, and I don't know any other way. If I'm getting the straight story from Reno, even the police can't tell where he is."

Chapter 15

I managed to get some sleep that night, but the next morning passed much too slowly. Edwin called to discuss a new course he was planning. I almost snapped at him, I was so frustrated and anxious to hear from Simon. By ten o'clock I was ready to pick up the phone and call him when an email appeared on my computer:

"Meredith: my friend is willing to see you, but only you. No cops, no companions. If you agree, come alone to meet us at my apartment at 7 p.m. tonight. – Simon"

I called Wynan.

"Not a chance, Red. You don't go into that neighborhood at night without me, and you don't go up to anyone's apartment alone either."

We argued for a few minutes, and then Wynan finally agreed. "Here's the deal. I drive you. I wait in the car for twenty minutes. If you don't come out by then, I go up to Gorshak's place and break down the door."

Thoughts of my meeting with Simon's friend almost made me forget I was scheduled to be the guest teacher in a news reporting class. As I entered the classroom, I noticed every chair was filled. It seemed no one was going to skip class since our topic was how to report on Danica Boerum's speech without letting your own bias show through the writing.

"I suppose this will be good practice on how to avoid using weighted words in news writing," said one of the students.

"And how to watch out for pejorative adjectives and nouns," said another.

"Just use her own words," I advised. "Enough of her direct quotes ought to give the readers or the listeners an idea of what kind of philosophy she represents."

"Is bigotry a philosophy?" one student cracked.

"Don't forget to charge up your cell phones so you can record everything. Don't rely exclusively on your notes or your memories." I turned to the wise cracker. "And tell me why you have already decided she's a bigot."

"I've been doing research on her."

"Research is good. Do as much as you can. What you've done so far should help you with today's in-class assignment. It's designed to help prepare you for the actual speech. So please get to your computers." The class moved over to the side of the room where a line of computers sat blinking. Some had brought laptops so they could stay at the classroom table and still file their stories to the main computer in the front of the room.

I began, "Today's assignment is to write a story on the impending appearance of Danica Boerum at the Purist parking lot. It's your job as reporters to provide enough information about her appearance so that your audience can decide for themselves whether or not they want to attend the speech."

"How do we politely describe her as a visiting racist?" The question came from a dark-haired girl at the end of the room.

"By not using the word racist, for starters."

The girl protested, "But how do I warn my readers that if they go to her speech, they're going to get a mega-dose of segregationist crap?"

"She's not a segregationist," said a Hispanic boy sitting next to her. "She doesn't want us be segregated. She wants us to be deported."

"That's what I mean about using her words rather than your opinions. This is a straight news story, folks. What you think doesn't matter. What you know does."

Several students began talking at once, and I had to call for quiet. "Stop talking and start thinking. Your job is to write an objective story about a woman's appearance at a student-sponsored event on this campus."

"It's not going to be easy."

"I never said it was going to be easy."

After class I returned to my office, determined to focus on my work instead of obsessing about my meeting with Simon that evening. I was supposed to join the provost at a student leadership gathering. Nell handed me my notes in time to get me out the door to head across campus. The day was chillier than before and the feel of the March wind blowing against my face was almost welcome. *Focus*, I said to myself as I buttoned my jacket and hurried up the stairs to a large conference room on the top floor of the student union building.

A group much larger than the one that had met in my office was gathered, some sitting in chairs around a large table, some standing against the wall. I recognized the president of the student council, plus several from the student government and a sizeable number of leaders of student groups, fraternities and sororities. This would be a good audience for Manny to address, and their numbers indicated their concern for the problem Boerum's appearance might pose.

Manny was standing at the head of the table, conferring with the student president and two women I knew led large sororities on campus. He turned from them and called the meeting to order, waving for me to join him at the head of the table.

"Thank you all for coming, and please thank the members of the faculty who excused you from classes. I have already been assured you will all be provided any make-up assignments necessary to cover your absence this afternoon."

The room grew absolutely quiet.

"As you know, we are all very concerned about the possibility of negative reactions to the appearance of Danica Boerum at the Purist assembly on their parking lot."

"Not just negative reactions," came a voice from the other end of the room. "Blood and bullets, more like."

"And that's exactly what we want to avoid," said Manny.

"So why not ban her ass from the campus?" came a female voice.

Manny looked exasperated but kept calm. "Because this is a university, and we don't ban speech just because we don't agree with what the speaker might say."

"Even if it causes violence?"

Several voices started up.

Manny held up his hand. "That's what we are gathered to discuss this afternoon: how to avoid violence."

More murmuring.

"Before I hear from you, I would like you to listen to an idea proposed by Meredith Solaris, the Dean of Journalism. She and I have been talking about this for some time, and I think she has a strategy that might be useful."

My eyes took in the crowded room. Fresh young faces in every color surrounded me. I realized how much I cherished the diversity on our campus. How in God's name were we supposed to ensure the safety of these beautiful children who had come here to be educated, not injured or insulted? But the decision had been made, and helping them figure their way through a brutal evening was the task at hand.

In my firmest voice, I said, "First of all, let me assure you I have absolutely no sympathy for the philosophy espoused by the American Purists or Danica Boerum. But I have done some research and talked to the Purists, and it's clear to me that they hope for something very dramatic to take place at their party."

"That's for damn sure," came the male voice again. I identified him as the head of one of the fraternities.

"Yes. But it can't happen, for damn sure. Because that's exactly what the Purists want. They want violence. They want bloodshed. That's what gets them lots of media coverage, and I think they honestly believe it helps them recruit more members to their cause."

"Jesus. How do we prevent that?"

"Well, here's my suggestion. If you and your friends decide to go—and I'm not saying not to go—remain polite and silent. If the speech is too much for you, get up and walk out quietly. If the Purists or any of Boerum's people taunt you, do not respond. Your best weapon against what she says and what she wants you to do in response, is no response at all. Just absolute silence."

As if to practice my advice, the room became unnaturally quiet. The expressions were cynical but the mouths were shut.

"What do you think?" I said.

Absolute silence.

"Do you like the idea?"

Silence again.

A few smiles around the table.

"Think this might work?"

A tentative nodding of a few heads.

"I can tell you for sure, your silence is getting to me."

Laughter and then a few comments to each other, none directed to me.

"Just for reassurance," Manny said, "there will be extra security guards inside and outside the tent. And I'll be there in front, although I may move toward the back if that's where anything starts up. So tell your friends and constituents if anyone tries to provoke you physically, any pushing and shoving or any attempt to prevent you from leaving, just signal a guard or me and we'll take care of it."

Finally, the fraternity president could remain quiet no longer. "Should we wear tape over our mouths?"

"No!" came in a chorus. "Let silence be a surprise."

"If you counsel enough of your friends, the Purists will probably hear about it ahead of time. And the speaker may try to goad you into making noise. But your silence may still have the desired effect. Without uttering fighting words, you may avoid a fight."

Manny walked me out to the campus path. "Good idea, Red. I have no idea if it will work, but I'm optimistic. You gave them a game to play, a contest to win, and we both know how much students love that. I hope Joe's making you a good dinner to reward you when you get home."

"Joe's gone on assignment. He hasn't been home for days."

Manny put his large arm around my shoulders. "Sorry, friend. That's lonely for you. Want to come to our house? Marguerite is making enchiladas."

"Oh, I wish I could. I love your wife's cooking. But I have an errand to run this evening that will probably keep me out late."

An errand, indeed. Wynan arrived ten minutes ahead of our agreed-upon time. It was clear his intention was to try to talk me out of seeing Simon and his lady friend alone.

"All I'm going to do is talk to her."

Wynan grunted as he opened the car door for me. He

slammed the door on his side for emphasis. "I don't know how I'm going to explain this to Joe when he gets back," he muttered.

"You probably won't have to explain it," I said as firmly as I could manage given my own discomfort. "C'mon, Wynan. The woman is a former prostitute, not an ax murderer. If she can help us get to Joe, it's worth whatever we have to do. The idea of Joe out there with no one to contact if he needs help makes my stomach hurt."

More grunting as we turned out of my driveway and headed into the dark. I knew Wynan was as worried as I was, and that was why he agreed to go along with my plan, disapproving grunts notwithstanding.

My thoughts shifted from Danica Boerum to Joe Morgan. Maybe I was being an idiot trying to find him myself. But I remembered the times Joe had found me just in time to prevent my getting killed or seriously injured. I never doubted it was my turn to help him. I just wasn't sure if I could. Joe had always followed his rescues of me with lectures about my taking stupid risks. It made him angry. And chances were he wasn't going to like the idea of my engaging the assistance of a former enemy.

I could almost see his eyes flash and imagine what he would have to say about this mission I had dragged Wynan into. But I was determined. After Joe's last time rescuing me, he had been furious, then forgiven me and announced the purchase of six weeks of self-defense training for me.

I obeyed reluctantly. I despise exercise and the self-defense classes were rigorous. The class was taught in a vacant storefront building in downtown Landry and it was always cold—even in summer, the old walls seems to hold onto the winter's chill. The instructor, a fifty-year-old ex-Marine whose body was made entirely of muscle and sinew as far as I could tell, put us through unrelenting combat exercises. I became acutely conscious that I was at least ten years older than any of the other women in the class. It took me forever to learn to kick hard upwards while lying down and then get up off the floor fast. Learning how to break a man's nose with my elbow took me an entire class, while everyone else moved on to even more vicious tactics. The instructor brought in football players dressed in puffy protective gear to teach us techniques to defend ourselves against enemies larger and stronger than ourselves. It took me all of those weeks to master the moves I needed to bring one of those guys to the ground, but I stuck with it.

As the lights of Reno loomed ahead, I decided I was grateful I had taken the course. After the lessons were over, Sadie asked me what I had learned. I thought for a minute and then said, "I think I have learned how to kill a man with my bare hands."

Chapter 16

"We're here," said Wynan, bringing me out of my reverie. The traffic to Reno had been light, so we found ourselves parked in front of Simon's apartment house at five minutes to seven. The street was deserted, the one streetlight near the corner the only illumination other than a few lit windows upstairs in the building. The entire first floor was occupied by a state welfare and social services office, closed and barred. No trees interrupted the sidewalk concrete. The beat of Latin music coming from one of the apartments was the only sound.

Wynan's face was grim in the dim light of the car. "Twenty minutes, Red. That's it. After that you'll hear me pounding at his door."

"I promise not to dawdle. Believe me, the prospective company is not that attractive."

"And remember, this woman may still be connected to the sex trade even if she's not working anymore. So be very cautious about how much you tell her about what you're looking for and why."

I took a deep breath. All this stress could not be good for the baby. "I promise. I'll be quick, careful and discreet."

The street was still dark and empty when I exited from Wynan's car. I opened an outer door and pushed a bell marked "Gorshak." A buzz came almost immediately. The stairs were lit with a harsh fluorescent light and covered with faded carpet that was ragged on the sides of the steps. Simon opened his door before I came to it and stood out in the hallway. He looked less dreary in a plaid shirt and slacks instead of his overcoat.

"Good evening, Meredith."

"Good evening," I whispered as he motioned me through the door.

The apartment was small and, except for a bright lamp on the desk, mostly in shadow. The windows were covered with shades and heavy curtains and the walls lined with bookshelves that reached from the floor to the ceiling. A desk confronted me as I made my way into the room. Piles of papers surrounded an ancient Mac computer that sat blinking at me. Beyond the desk, I could make out a heavy leather couch and two upholstered chairs.

A light switched on by one of the chairs. Curled up against the faded upholstery was a thin woman with gray blonde hair pulled back in a ponytail. Her long red-nailed fingers held a lit cigarette and she brushed ashes from the front of a black sweater.

"Veronica, this is Meredith. Meredith, Veronica."

The woman did not get up or hold out her hand, just nodded and gave me a steady stare as I sat in the chair opposite her.

"Thank you for seeing me, Veronica."

Veronica drew deeply on her cigarette and blew out a stream of smoke toward Simon, now seated on the couch. "You sure she's not a cop?" Her tone was gravelly, betraying years of tobacco.

"I'm sure, Veronica," he said, with more patience than I had ever heard from him before. "As I told you, Meredith is a professor. She and I taught together a while ago at the university."

Her eyes fastened on me. "How come you're interested in what I have to say? I don't know nothing about much anymore. Not enough to interest a fancy lady college professor."

"I need help finding someone important to me, and my hope is you may be able to tell me where to look."

Long draw on the cigarette, balancing an extended ash until, at the last minute, she flicked it into a tiny metal ashtray teetering on the arm of the chair. I noticed burn holes on the fabric of the arm. I suspected this was not Veronica's first time in Simon's apartment.

"A man or a kid?" Her eyes were steady and humorless.

Good. Simon had not told her anything about my mission.

"Both actually, but first, the man."

She tossed her head back and gave a snort. "A man. Of course. No woman who looks like you should have to go chasing after some bozo. What'd he do? Dump you? Or steal from you?"

In spite of Wynan's cautions, I took a chance. "He got me pregnant."

Both of them gasped. She jutted out her chin. "Shit. And you want to find him? Why? To get him back or to make him pay?"

"I'm not sure yet. First I have to find him and tell him."

Veronica drew another long pull on her cigarette, never taking her eyes off me. She did not look friendly or sympathetic, but something in her gaze told me she was, at the very least, interested. After a long pause, she exhaled, the smoke plume rising toward the dim ceiling. "And what makes you think I can help you?"

"He's a pimp."

That brought an ironic smile. "You've got to be shitting me. A woman like you has unprotected sex with a pimp and gets knocked up?"

I pretended to look ashamed, even tried to blush. "He's a

really attractive man, and I didn't know he was a pimp when I dated him."

She put her head back and gave another snort that sounded like a rooting pig.

"Black, brown or white?"

"White."

"What else can you tell me about him?"

"Tall, well-built, dark hair. Green eyes."

Veronica stubbed out her cigarette and sat forward, elbows on her knees, scrutinizing me. Her eyes were beady, but not unkind, and I could see deep wrinkles in her cheeks. Smoker's face.

"I don't suppose you know his real name."

"He gave me a name, but now I doubt it was real."

"That's okay. Green eyes and tall will have to do."

"Can you help me?"

She tossed her head in the direction of Simon, who had risen from the couch and was standing by the window. "This man Gorshak here has been good to me, helped me out any number of times and never asked for a favor until now. I'll see what I can find out, but if it's tricky you may have to cough up some money."

"I can give you a hundred now."

She nodded. "That'll do for starters. Let me see what I can find out."

All Wynan said when I got back in the car was "Good. Fast work." As we drove out of Reno, I told him word for word what had been said in Simon's apartment.

A slow chuckle emerged. "You told her that the man got you pregnant? Wait 'til Joe hears that."

He would soon, I hoped, but kept that thought to myself. "I

was trying to keep her interested enough to help me. Seemed like a good thing to say at the time."

Another chuckle. "You should have been a detective, Red. You do have the instincts."

"I was an investigative reporter before I went into teaching. That probably helped. But I don't want to be a detective. I'm happier being a detective's girlfriend."

Wynan dropped me off in front of my house and delivered a parting shot as I opened the car door. "You know not to trust either of these people, right? Especially if they ask for a lot more money."

"I know, Wynan. But we need help to find Joe if he's still alive, and these people might be able to provide it."

His eyes squinted. "Don't worry so much, sweetheart. Joe's still alive. I'd bet on it."

But, of the six messages on my answering machine, not one was from Joe. Four were from faculty, full of concern about Boerum's appearance. The last one from Phyllis almost made me cry—I was already close to tears when I entered my house and found only my dog to greet me. Her voice trembled.

"Red, I know you plan to go to that damned speech tomorrow night, but please, please be careful. People are going to get hurt, and I don't want one of them to be you. You're too important to me."

I walked into the kitchen, gave Charlie his food and brewed myself a strong cup of tea. I sat at the kitchen table, sipping and wondering if I could work up any appetite for dinner. Charlie came over and put his soft head on my knee. His brown eyes looked up at me, entreating. He missed Joe as much as I did. I stroked his fur.

"He'll be back soon. He always comes home, right? And

when I tell him about the baby he'll be happy, won't he? He's a good man. He likes kids. He loves me."

Charlie nuzzled the side of my leg.

"For Christ's sake, Charlie, the man is thirty-nine years old. By the time the baby's born, he'll be forty. It's time he settled down. It's time he started a family, right?"

Charlie's chin came back on my knee as if to signal agreement. I resumed stroking his fur.

The phone rang.

"See you got home safely," said Simon.

"I did. Thank you again for introducing me to Veronica."

"Glad to help. Ronnie's gone out to check out a few possible leads. If she gets any information about your green-eyed fellow she'll call in the morning. Nice story about him being a pimp. Even I was convinced at first. But it was good for her, because she has no use for cops. And undercover cops especially."

Oh, Jesus, Simon had figured it out. My heart rate increased. "What makes you think I'm looking for a cop?"

"I know you are. And given your desperation, I figure it's that Morgan person. The part about the green eyes clued me in. But don't fret. I didn't mention anything to Ronnie to scare her off. I'll keep your confidence."

No point attempting deception. "Thank you, Simon."

"I do like the sound of thanks coming from you, Meredith. By the way, are you really pregnant?"

Had I really come to trust my old enemy? It seemed so. "Yes. I am. But it's still a secret, and the Morgan person doesn't know yet. It's one of the reasons I need to find him."

"Good enough reason, I guess. Ronnie will do her best. So congratulations and get some sleep. We'll talk in the morning."

Chapter 17

Simon's word was good. The phone rang at eight thirty the following morning just as I was about to leave for school. Simon put Veronica on the phone.

"I think I may know where your deadbeat guy is," she said, her voice low and hoarse.

"That's great, Veronica. May I call you Ronnie?"

"Sure. Anyhow, this girl I meet for coffee sometimes after she's finished working told me about a tall dark-haired guy, with eyes like emeralds, she said."

I could hardly breathe. "That sounds like my guy. When did she see him?"

"She didn't say, just that she thinks he's good-looking and that he works for one of the pimps in Reno. He drives a van and brings girls up from Cali and Vegas."

"Does that give you any idea of where he might be?"

I could hear her inhale. "I think I know where this pimp keeps his girls when they're not out on the job. But I have to tell you, honey, he is one mean mother. You don't want to mess with him. Also, I don't know when your Green Eyes works for him or what days he's in Reno."

"Could we go to the place where this pimp keeps his girls?"

Long pause.

"I really need to find this guy, Ronnie. Do you think you can help?"

Another long pause. "Maybe...maybe. But just you and me. No one else can come with us. Not Simon, and not that black dude I saw you driving away with last night."

"I promise it will just be me."

"Another thing. We're gonna have to dress you up like a working girl. You go into that neighborhood looking like you did last night and they'll be sure you're police or a social worker. Either way, they'll scatter, and if you ask a lot of questions, you could get hurt bad."

The idea of dressing like a prostitute confounded me. What would I have to wear? Fishnet stockings and a low-cut top? Too much mascara and lipstick? I was embarrassed to even think about it.

Oh well, I had meetings to get through before I could take off for Reno and find out what Veronica had in mind. We agreed to get together at Simon's apartment at four and start our search as soon as it was dark outside.

Nell was bustling when I got to the office. She and Wynan had settled on a small country inn with a large courtyard lined with maple trees that would turn a blazing orange for their October wedding. She was pushing paper around her desk, making neat piles and setting up file folders for all the elements of her ceremony.

"Are you planning on bridesmaids?" I asked, enjoying her flushed face and the excitement in her eyes.

She stopped, hands poised on a pile of folders. "I was thinking of asking you and Sadie to be my bridesmaids. My daughter-in-law is going to stand up for me as matron of honor."

Dear Nell. I knew she was going to do that. I was happy that she considered Sadie as good a friend as she considered me. I was glad to say yes, but not ready to tell her I would probably be conspicuously pregnant by October. "What colors do you want us to wear?"

"Well, my daughter-in-law wants to wear lavender, so I was wondering how you'd feel about you and Sadie wearing purple." She bit her lower lip, the first sign of apprehension I had seen.

"I can't speak for Sadie, but think I would love to be in a royal color. Suitable to my status, don't you think?"

"Not to mention your hair color, your highness." She smiled back.

Much as I wanted to hang on to that moment of frivolous girl talk and avoid all the serious stuff, my conscience took over. "What's on the schedule this morning?"

"Editorial staff from the student paper are due here in fifteen minutes, and that detective Norman O'Hare wants to see you at eleven."

"Did he say why?"

"Nope. Just wants a few minutes."

Rosie's news staff was clearly feeling a bit rudderless with their leader still stuck in the hospital.

"I think we'll know how to cover the speech okay," said the assistant editor, a stocky boy with dark curly hair. "But I really want to try to get an interview with Boerum and Rosie has forbidden that. She said absolutely not. She thinks the woman is too dangerous and that her interview with Boerum is what put her in the hospital. Although we can't figure out why."

Obviously, Rosie had told her staff about questioning Boerum on Los Angeles when she met with them in her hospital room.

I sympathized with their eagerness to be thorough, but agreed with Rosie. "None of us is sure why Boerum would have set an attack dog on Rosie, or even if he is part of Boerum's staff. But Rosie was shot hours after her telephone interview, and since she almost died, she and, for that matter, I would prefer you stay away from trying for any personal approaches to the woman."

The boy looked annoyed.

"I know. It would make a better story if you could get some information that helped explain Boerum and her beliefs, but Rosie's right. Stay away from her and her assistants as well."

"How about interviewing some of the Purists on campus?" asked a girl wearing frameless glasses.

"Take your best shot," said the curly-haired boy before I could answer. "They clam up when you even try to get anything substantial out of them."

I remembered my visit with the Purist vice president. The boy was right, but I appreciated the frustration I saw in front of me. We had trained these students to be hard-charging journalists, yet violence had intruded and made us timid. Damn, I hated that.

"Do as much research as you can and make sure your readers have a clear picture of what she actually said and how the crowd reacted. You'll get a good story." And, I prayed, a non-violent one.

The group filed out, muttering to themselves.

I called after them, "Remember, you run a prize-winning student newspaper. Make me proud. Make Rosie proud."

At eleven, Norman O'Hare filled the doorway to my office.

"Coffee?" I said, motioning him to a large chair near the couch.

"No thanks," he said, easing his bulk into the chair and looking solemn.

"What's up?" I asked, dreading bad news about Joe.

"We think we might have identified the man who attacked Rosie Jenkins."

"That's good, isn't it?"

"Yeah," he shifted in his chair, "but we don't think he works for Boerum. We think he might be a grad student here at the U."

"Really? Who?"

"We don't have a firm ID yet, but if he's a student here, that suggests the shooting may have been about something personal. Maybe an old boyfriend or someone who wanted to be Rosie's boyfriend and got turned down."

"Rosie doesn't have a boyfriend right now. She was dating someone last year. Could it have been him?"

"Rosie says no. Last year's boyfriend graduated and got a tech job in China. We checked him out and he's still in Beijing."

"So why..."

"Because one of the tenants came upon this guy fooling around with the buzzers in the entrance to the apartment building, and he asked which apartment belonged to Jenkins."

"And the tenant thought he was a student?"

"The guy was wearing a backpack and said he was answering an ad offering to sell a couch. He was big, older than most students, but dressed in a football jersey. That's why the tenant thought he might be a grad student here."

"And, of course, Rosie doesn't have a couch for sale."

"Right."

"Did the tenant describe the man?"

"Vaguely. Like I said, big. Dark-haired. Maybe in his forties."

"A number of men on campus fit that. Did Rosie say she knew anyone like that?"

"She said no one came to mind, but she wasn't sure. As you say, a number of men fit that description. That's one of the reasons I'm on campus, Red. Unless you can think of who the guy might be, I'm heading up to the graduate school office to go through some of their files and see if I can get any photos for the tenant to look at."

"Did the graduate director agree? Those files are confidential."

"Oh, yeah. Most people at Mountain West cooperate when a crime has been committed. I rarely have to get a subpoena."

He looked uncomfortable but made no move to leave.

"Norm, what's the other reason you're here?"

"The Chief asked me to stop in while I was on campus...it's about Joe."

I inhaled and blew out air so forcibly I made a whistling sound. "What about him?"

"We haven't been able to find him. I mean, Landry and Reno PD haven't."

I could almost hear my heart beating. "Do you think something's happened?"

Norm's face got heavier. "We don't know, Red, but the Chief wanted me to tell you that we're putting together a joint task force, Reno and Landry, and preparing for a full press search tomorrow in every neighborhood we know has sex traffickers."

"Whoa. Won't that much activity drive them underground?"

He looked away and rubbed his hands together nervously. "Maybe. But I think our chief wants to try everything. He can't bear the idea of losing..." Norm's eyes grew wet and so did mine.

I put my hand over his. He rose and gave me a hug. "Don't worry, Red. We'll find him."

After Norm left, I remained in the chair. Police pouring into the neighborhoods might make things worse for Joe. Now more than ever, I was sure it was imperative I look for Joe tonight.

Without Wynan. Not just because he would support the police effort and oppose my going into danger, but because Veronica had been adamant. *Come alone. Just you.*

Chapter 18

I stopped off at Rosie's apartment on my way to the hospital for a short visit before leaving for Reno. Norm had been helpful enough to give me the keys and permission to pick up some of Rosie's things to make her more comfortable during her hospital stay. Police tape still clung to the door but did not prevent my entry. I had been to the tiny one-room studio apartment once before, so I knew what it was supposed to look like. An appalling sight met me when I walked into the room. What little furniture Rosie had was upended and one of the lighter chairs had been smashed into pieces. Her bed was tossed, the drawers to her bureau pulled out and emptied on the floor. Her clothes were everywhere.

It didn't make sense. It was obvious Rosie didn't have anything worth stealing. The only way one could explain the chaos was to assume the intruder had meant Rosie's attack to look like the result of a robbery.

In the bathroom I found a few of the things she had asked for and her robe was still hanging on the door. I gathered them up and left, calling Nell on my cell phone. "We need to get a crew over to Rosie's apartment as soon as the police give us permission. It's a mess here."

*   *   *

At the hospital, the older police guard was dozing by the door. I gave his foot a nudge and he looked up, apologetic.

"That girl's still in danger, you know," I said, without looking at him.

He cleared his throat and shifted his weight. "I'm on it, miss. Don't worry."

But I worried about everything as I knocked on Rosie's door.

Rosie was not in her bed.

"Rosie?"

A voice came from behind the table against the wall. Rosie peeked round. She was on her knees holding an electrical cord. "Trying to get the damn laptop plugged in," she said, returning to her task.

"Rosie, for Christ's sake, get back into bed this minute."

Rosie got up and walked back to the bed. "I'm fine, Red, honestly. I told them they could let me out of here, but they insisted I stay through the weekend. I'm going nuts, and I really want to hear that speech tomorrow night."

"Maybe it will be televised," I said, plumping pillows behind her back.

"Not a chance. I checked. But one of my friends in my video class thinks he might be able to rig up his camera and a live feed from the Purist tent. At least he's going to try."

"You should be concentrating on getting well, not on Danica Boerum's speech."

"I've got to figure her out. The more I think about it, the more I believe she had something to do with the creep who attacked me. I can feel it."

"Norm came by this morning and told me about a big man fussing with the buzzers to your apartments."

Rosie scowled. "Yeah. Norm was here too. I don't know any guys like that, but he was well-built, Norm says, and could have been the one who was wearing a ski mask who beat the shit out of me and trashed my place before I escaped and ran down the stairs."

"And then he followed and shot you."

"Yeah. When I tried to get away after he grabbed me again. He got pissed because I wouldn't let him drag me into his black van."

"Have you remembered enough to know if you could identify him?"

"Yeah, I remember his smell. Sweat and some sickening cologne. And I remember he had a heavy gold chain around his neck."

"You've told Norm?"

"I tell Norm everything. Norm's become my surrogate father."

I drove to Reno full of dread. My hands were trembling and my head ached. The familiar route was agonizingly slow. A traffic jam outside of the city brought on a wave of nausea I had to fight back. This was just the sort of act that drove Joe insane: my taking a truly dangerous risk. Taking off on my own with no Joe and no Wynan to protect me. Ready to depend on a woman I had known for only one day and a man who used to hate me. And now it wasn't just me at risk. What was I thinking?

I took a deep breath. *Stop this nonsense. You're strong and capable and smart and you're doing what you need to do for the sake of your family.*

Family. Now there was a word that made me smile. That was the word that my aunt, Evangeline, had used when she called from Sacramento. "How are you and your growing family?" she had asked, her voice cheerful and full of affection.

"I think the baby's fine, but I haven't had a chance to tell his father yet. Joe's still undercover in Reno."

"Are you taking your pre-natal vitamins and eating fresh food?"

Evangeline sounded a bit like Sadie, and I appreciated her taking a parental role. We talked for a few more minutes, agreeing she would visit in a few weeks when Sacramento State had its spring break.

"I hope you don't mind, but I would love to be close to my brother's grandchild."

I didn't mind. Not one bit.

"Well, you take care now. I'm counting on everything to be wonderful."

So was I.

It was still light when I parked on the street in front of Simon's apartment building. I reached into the backseat to grab a pair of high-heeled boots Veronica had suggested I bring. "I don't think you and I have the same shoe size," she had said.

Both of them were waiting for me in the apartment. Simon offered to make me a cup of tea while Veronica began examining the boots and then pulled open a suitcase of clothes she had brought over, holding garments up to my shoulders to gauge a likely fit.

Half an hour later I looked in the mirror in Simon's bedroom. I was wearing a red miniskirt and my boots. No net stockings. "You go barelegged on this job," Veronica had said.

A cheap black rayon tee was stretched over my expanding breasts and cut low to reveal several inches of cleavage, barely covering the nipples. A pink shrug barely covered my arms. A black silky purse hung over one shoulder. I had to say I looked amazingly like the hooker I was supposed to be. But it was discomfiting. I had to push away doubts about my mission.

"Now the makeup and hair," said Veronica, taking my arm and leading me into the bathroom. Another twenty minutes while Veronica applied makeup: mascara, eyeshadow and liner and a lipstick color I had never before seen, much less worn. Then she sprinkled some glittery stuff on my eyelids and teased my hair into a helmet. I looked again in the mirror.

Unbelievable. A woman for sale, no doubt about it.

She sent me back into Simon's living room while she dressed herself. I sat tentatively on the edge of a kitchen chair, sipping tea and trying not to smudge any of Veronica's work.

"I wish you would let me go with you," said Simon. His gray head was bowed and his bony hands rubbed back and forth across his knees.

Still overwhelmed by the risk I was about to take, I decided to trust Simon with another mission. "Do you know where Veronica is taking me?"

"I know the house she thinks your guy is in."

I looked steadily at Simon's gray eyes. Where I once saw hatred, now I saw sympathy. "If Ronnie and I are not back in an hour, would you be willing to call the police and give them that address?"

His head went down and his hands started to tremble. "Ronnie won't like that idea."

"I know she won't, but Simon, I need backup of some kind. I can't call Wynan. It's too late and he's an hour away."

"Okay. Just don't ever tell Ronnie I agreed to this."

I reached into my handbag and gave him the card the Reno Police Chief had given to me. "This is the chief's direct line. Use my name. He'll know what I'm trying to do even if he disapproves of it."

A ghost of a smile appeared on Simon's face. "Oh, I'm sure

he'll disapprove. Christ, Red, I disapprove. Ronnie may know her way around here, but you're a civilian, kid. I know how to use a gun even if I'm ancient. So I still wish you would let me at least tag along."

"Well, you can't. One sight of you with the two of us and they won't even open the door," said Veronica emerging from the bathroom dressed in tight pants and top with only a little less makeup than mine. Her gray blond hair was covered with a curly dark brown wig that set off her eyes. Clearly she had been striking when she was younger.

Simon smiled weakly. "Well, I'd hire either one of you for an evening."

"That's my boy," said Veronica, planting a kiss on the top of his head and then turning to me. "You ready to walk out, missy?"

I stood up, tottering a bit on the heels of my boots. Simon grabbed my elbow and then walked me to his desk. He opened the drawer. A small revolver sat in the center. "Put this in your little black purse," he said, handing me the gun. "I'll feel better knowing you have it."

"Thank you."

"You do know how to use that, don't you?" Simon leaned closer to me. I could feel the heat of his breath.

"I know how," I said. Joe had taught me to shoot at the range outside of Landry. Teaching me how to use a gun along with the self-defense lessons had been Joe's way of coping with my tendency to take risks. I guess he'd figured I was incurable. He'd been right.

Veronica grabbed my arm and headed me toward the door. "C'mon, let's go get this deadbeat dad."

The night was chilly and the pink shrug did not provide any warmth. Veronica kept her hand on my arm as we walked away from the apartment building.

"Walk faster and swing your hips a little. You're walking like a schoolteacher instead of a working girl."

"I am a schoolteacher."

She gave one of her snorts. "Try not to look like one."

We passed more apartment buildings and came to a corner with a delicatessen and a blinking sign indicating an emergency clinic one flight up above the store. Two men with short beards, both dressed in jeans and leather jackets, were leaning against the door to the deli. Their eyes never left us as we approached. "Evening, ladies," said the older of the two. "You here to show us a good time?"

"Not tonight," snapped Veronica. "We have an important errand to run."

"Ooh, important errand. How about that. Nice tits on your red-haired friend. You bring her back this way, okay?" His eyes bugged out at me.

"Oh, mama. I'll pay double for you," said the younger man, grinding his hips in my direction.

The light changed and Veronica half dragged me across the street and away from the two men.

"I guess I passed," I said.

"Of course you passed. I know how to doll a girl up nice. Just stay in the game when we get to the next block."

I shivered against the March wind and noticed my nipples had reacted to the chill and were obvious against the thin material of the t-shirt top.

The apartment buildings were replaced by a line of frame houses set only a few feet apart and separated by scrubby patches of grass and gravel and chain-link fences. "Beware of Dog" signs were attached to each one and the sound of barking drowned out the click of our heels on the sidewalk.

We turned the corner and came to a house slightly larger than its neighbors set back from the sidewalk by a concrete parking pad. Veronica stopped. "This is it. This is where Green Eyes is supposed to work."

I looked up at the two-story house. Lights were on in every window and the sound of music came from inside. The house was shabby and in need of a paint job. Facing the street was a small front porch and a set of steps down to the concrete pad. I sensed the movement of people behind the curtains but could not actually see anyone, just shadows against the lights.

"You're sure you want to do this?" Veronica was looking at the door to the house.

I felt a shudder not related to the cold air. I gripped the little black bag to feel the hard shape of the revolver. "I'm sure," I said. The possibility of seeing Joe overcame my fear.

The door to the house opened. "We've been spotted," said Veronica. "Let me do the talking."

An enormous man stepped out under the porch light. He must have been six foot six with a massive torso encased in a tight satin shirt. He walked toward us, the muscles in his shoulders moving in a rolling pattern. His hair was thick and black and his eyes dark brown. He looked for all the world like a large male version of Danica Boerum, only twice as frightening. Maybe Rosie was right and the Boerum family was in more than one business.

The man stopped and surveyed us. A slight grin revealed a front tooth made of gold. It matched a gold chain that hung down the front of the open shirt. He circled around us and came back to face us. "What brings you here, Ronnie? You trying to sell this bitch?"

He transferred his gaze from Veronica to me and looked me over slowly and carefully.

"Nice, but a little old for my customers," he said, grinning and flashing his gold tooth among startling white teeth. His large fingers twisted the chain hanging down in the gap in his shirt. "But I wouldn't mind doing her myself. What's your name, Red?"

"Patty," I said, giving the name Veronica had told me to use.

He whistled through his teeth. "Patty Cake. Patty Cake. Baker's man. Bake me a cake as fast as you can. Well, darlin', I'm the baker's man for you." He ran two fingers down my neck and into the front of my shirt between my breasts. I winced. But I felt his sexual power. This was how a pimp worked.

"Leave her be for now, Al," Veronica said softly. "She needs to see one of your drivers. Tall dude with green eyes."

The man withdrew his hand and his smile. His voice turned icy. "What she *need* to see him for?"

"Something they have to settle between them. Is he here?"

Al cupped my breasts with his hands and breathed hot sour air into my face. "So, Patty Cake," his voice velvet again, "what will I get in return for getting your tall dude out here?"

I stifled my gag reflex. "Whatever you want, baby. Whatever you want."

The toothy smile came back and he turned toward the house. From the back his shoulders looked even broader than before and his legs encased in tight pants were massive and muscled.

"Jesus, what do I do if he comes back?"

There was a disturbing note of uncertainty in Veronica's reply. "Let's cross that bridge when we come to it."

We stood in the darkness for what felt like an eternity. Then the door opened again and a surprising version of Joe Morgan stepped under the porch light. He was dressed in the same kind of satin shirt the first man had worn, open to the waist, a gold chain against his chest. He peered into the darkness. When he saw me, he staggered for a moment, then regained his balance and strode forward.

"What the hell are you doing here?" His hand clamped down on my shoulder. "What's this get-up? And who's this woman?"

Veronica stepped away into the darkness behind her, leaving Joe and me alone, facing each other on the sidewalk.

"She's helping me. I had to find you, Joe. Your contact has been injured, he's in the hospital."

"I know. He was stabbed in a fight. Why in the name of God would the chief send you to tell me that?"

I put my hand on his shoulder just to touch him. "He didn't send me. I came on my own."

Joe pulled away. "Shit, Red. Why? You could get both of us killed."

"I know. But I had to know you were alive, and I have to tell you that Norm O'Hare told me both departments, Landry and Reno, are going to sweep the neighborhoods tomorrow to find you."

Joe looked agonized. "That'll drive them to ground and they'll take the girls with them. You have to get out of here and tell them to back off."

"When can you get out of this?"

"I was going to try for tomorrow, but I need time to set things up if I am going to bring Snowbird out with me."

"So you found her."

"Yeah, but just yesterday. Red, you have to get to the chief. Tell him to cancel the search. Instead, tell him to send in a small, and I mean small, force at five thirty tomorrow afternoon. A shipment is coming in then. The house will be full of illegal Asian girls, all underage. They can make a good bust if they don't screw up and put these bastards on alert." He looked around to make sure no one else had come out of the house.

Al's face appeared in the window. Joe took a step closer. "Red, you have to get out of here now. Back off and yell something at me. And, honey, I'm sorry, I'm going to have to hit you in the face and tell you to leave and not come back. Al has to believe we've had a fight."

"Joe, I..."

"Now, Red. Now."

I backed away. "You lousy bastard," I screamed at him.

His hand struck my face so hard I almost fell into the street. Then he turned and shouted over his shoulder, "And don't come back, bitch. Ever."

Veronica's hand appeared from behind me and tugged at my elbow. "We gotta leave now. Before Al decides to come out and collect his fee."

That frightened me enough to move quickly with Veronica down the street and away into the night.

Chapter 19

Even before he came into his office, I could hear the Reno Police Chief's voice shouting at one of his men about being dragged away from the dinner table to "talk to some hooker who wouldn't talk to anyone else."

My cheek was still red and my jaw still ached from the force of Joe's slap. I had left Veronica on the sidewalk next to my car in front of Simon's apartment house. "Thank you. Thank you," I said, giving her a quick hug. "Please give this gun back to Simon. It makes me nervous."

"Don't you want to come upstairs and change back into your clothes?"

"Not now. First I have a message to deliver."

Annoyance covered her face. "To the cops, right? Your dude is undercover."

"I'm sorry, Veronica. I would have liked to trust you but I wasn't sure. I hope I can trust you now. His life depends upon you keeping his secret."

She took a deep breath and then put her hands on my shoulders, "You can, but you were right, Meredith. You shouldn't trust me or any other folks you don't know. Not in this town. But you can trust me with this. I won't spill. It's time Big Al got his. He's mean to his girls. As far as that raid goes, my mouth stays shut. That goes for your green-eyed cop too."

"Thank you, Ronnie. For everything. I'll come back for my clothes later if that's okay."

"Come when you can. Simon doesn't go to bed until midnight." I wondered for a brief moment just how she knew that. "Take your time. I just worry you'll have a hard time getting through to the Chief looking like you do."

"I have to do this as soon as possible."

"Good luck. See you later."

The Reno Police Chief stood in the doorway of his office staring at me. Then recognition. "Dr. Solaris?"

"Yes, Chief. It's me. I'm dressed like this because I went looking for Joe Morgan."

"You did what?"

"I dressed like a prostitute to go look for Joe Morgan."

"Holy shit, lady. You could have gotten yourself killed."

"I know. But I found him and he gave me a message for you."

The Chief walked toward his desk, his eyes still fastened on me.

"You could have blown his cover and gotten both of you shot, you know."

"I know. But I was careful not to blow his cover. He's fine."

"Whew. I thought Morgan was reckless, but his girlfriend...Jesus, you college professors are something else."

"I'm sorry, Chief, but I knew someone in the neighborhood where Joe is, and I thought I could help." I tried to look as humble and contrite as possible.

The chief scowled. "What's the message?"

I handed him a piece of his own notepaper I had appropriated from his desk while I waited for him. "Joe says to call off the search party or you'll drive the ring away with their girls. He says to instead send a small squad to this address at five thirty tomorrow afternoon. He says the pimp in that house is expecting a delivery of underage girls and that you could make a good bust."

"Whose house is it?"

"Somebody named Al. A big man."

The Chief picked up his phone and called for a detective to join us. "This is Henry Jankowski, head of our sex crimes division."

Henry was muscular and young. He gave me a tentative smile.

"Henry, this is Dr. Meredith Solaris. She's normally the dean of the journalism school at Mountain West. Tonight she dressed as a hooker and went undercover to find her boyfriend, Joe Morgan."

Jankowski's jaw dropped. "You really look the part, Dr. Solaris. Did you find him?" The Chief handed Jankowski my note. "Great. Morgan's a good cop. Whose house?"

"Al. Big man."

"I'll be damned. Big Al, a.k.a. Big Daddy Al, a.k.a. Alistair Boerum. All the way here from LA. Wonder why?"

Oh my God.

"Is Big Al related to Danica Boerum?"

"The Purist woman? The one giving a speech tomorrow night at your school?"

"Yes, that woman."

Jankowski shrugged. "I dunno. I never connected the two of them, but if he is, it might explain why he's come up here from LA. Although I've never known a pimp to be much interested in politics."

Oh, Rosie. How right you were.

"I have a student newspaper editor who was once trafficked in LA and says she knows a woman who looks like Danica Boerum from there."

The Chief frowned. "I suppose it's possible, but I have a hard time seeing a right-wing politico and a big-time pimp from LA having much in common."

"Unless they're family," I said.

"Well, we've never had reason to check her out or determine where she came from. But the idea that an LA pimp would be related to a Purist speaker seems a stretch."

The Chief was right. It didn't make sense. But Rosie had been attacked by a man who fit Big Al's description, attacked for a reason—even if it didn't make sense yet.

"A man who attacked the student I mentioned fits his description."

"That's odd," said Jankowski. "The only students Big Al is usually interested in are eighth graders."

I left Jankowski and the Chief planning the next day's raid on Big Al's House and drove back to Simon's. As predicted, he was still up, only now wearing a robe and slippers.

Veronica was curled in one of the easy chairs watching television and sipping whiskey, straight, no ice. She was wearing a chenille robe and her hair was falling around her shoulders. So that's how it was.

I changed back into my clothes and removed the makeup Veronica had so generously slathered on my face. With my arms full of my boots and handbag, it was hard hugging them goodnight and thanking them again and again. When I finally left, Veronica was back in her chair, Simon perched on the armrest, his head inclined her way and his shoulder touching hers.

Seeing Simon Gorshak happy was almost more than I could comprehend. My mind filled with thoughts of Joe. I touched the cheek he had slapped and started home, trying not to weep as I drove through the dark streets, headed for the highway to Landry.

Joe in a satin shirt and a gold chain. Joe, alive and whole, but tough and distant from me. Joe, who still didn't know about the child I carried.

Two years ago, he had rescued me from the hands of an enraged professor who tried to kill me. Last fall, he had found me bound and gagged in a strange house and saved me again. My risk-taking had almost broken us up, but not quite.

"It was my turn to rescue you," I had wanted to say, but there hadn't been time. It had all gone down so quickly. No time to tell him about my pregnancy. No time to tell him I loved him.

The lights along the highway raced past. I slowed down a bit. No more speeding for me. I touched my cheek and thought of all the nights Joe's hands had touched me with incredible gentleness. My mind flooded with thoughts of Joe's mouth on my neck, Joe's fingers in my hair, Joe inside of me.

I almost missed the turn off to Landry.

The next morning, the Nevada weather turned warm again. The sun shone in through the kitchen window. Charlie danced around his bowl while I prepared his breakfast. "I saw Joe last night, Charlie. He's alive and okay and I think he might come home soon."

Charlie danced faster. I'm sure he recognized the word "Joe" and that was all he needed to celebrate.

I poured myself a cup of coffee, telephoned Wynan and confessed. There was a long silence.

"You're all right?"

"Yes, I'm fine. So is Joe, even if he's trapped in that house for a few more hours."

"Now I understand why Joe gets so angry with you. What you did was insane."

"Dammit, Wynan, it was the only way to get through to Joe without blowing his cover and putting him in danger."

"It was clever, I'll say that. But the only way? I doubt I'll ever think so. And I doubt Joe will ever think so."

"Well, you two can discuss that when you see him later." I told Wynan about the plan to raid the house at five thirty.

"I already knew about it," said Wynan. "I got a call ten minutes ago telling me the Landry force is going to sit tight and let Reno deal with this. They just didn't tell me about your part in all this."

"I think we should be there."

"What? Now I know you've gone 'round the bend."

"No, I mean it, Wynan. I want to see this happen. I want to see Joe as soon as I can. I have something really important to tell him that I couldn't talk about last night."

"What's so important?"

"I can't tell you yet."

"You better tell me, or you and I are not going anywhere."

I caved. "I'm going to have a baby. Joe and I are going to have a baby. He doesn't know yet. I have to see him and tell him as soon as I can."

The sound of Wynan's laughter was so loud over the phone, Charlie heard it and perked up his ears.

"And you want to go to Reno to observe a police raid? Just so you can tell Joe you're pregnant? Must be the hormones. That's nuts, Red. What if things don't go well? What if there's gunplay? C'mon, lady, get smart."

"I mean it, Wynan. We can park down the street away from the house. Out of range."

But Wynan would not bend. "Even if it comes off smoothly, the police will have to arrest Joe along with all the others in the house. They have to maintain his cover. Revealing him as an undercover cop could get him killed later. So you won't be able to talk to him. You won't be able to tell him anything. Not until tomorrow or even the next day."

Wynan would not bend, but neither would I.

"Okay. I wanted to be with you. But if I have to go by myself..."

"Shit. You're impossible."

"I'm pregnant, Wynan. I get to be impossible."

After another fifteen minutes of my being adamant and Wynan being stubborn, he agreed to pick me up at four at the journalism school.

Nell followed me into my office and closed the door.

"Wynan and I have breakfast together, you know. We talk." Her hands were on her hips, her mouth a straight line. Then a brilliant smile. "A baby. Oh, Red, how wonderful." My guess was Wynan had not told her the rest of my news or about last night's adventure.

"I wanted to tell you, but..."

"I know. You haven't had a chance to tell Joe yet. But you will after this raid is over."

So Wynan had told her everything.

Her arms went around me. "I think what Joe is doing is heroic and you, my friend, are incredibly courageous. But then, you always have been." Nell's enthusiasm got me. I never thought of myself as courageous, because I was usually consumed with self-doubt. But her endorsement went a long way in cheering me up.

"So you're not going to try to talk me out of the trip to Reno this afternoon?"

"I'm not. You deserve to be in on the arrests after the risk you took. You know Joe will give you hell about this when he sees you. But at the very least you should get to hold him in your arms and let him thank God and thank you for finding him." Nell's eyes were shining as she released me.

"Wynan's not sure I'll even be able to talk to Joe until long after he's been arrested with the others."

"At least you'll know he's safe."

Maybe she had been able to reassure her fiancé. Like Joe, Wynan Congers was a traditionalist when it came to following a woman's lead. Come what may, Nell was ever my champion.

"So, in the meantime, what's on the schedule between now and when he and I leave for Reno?"

"Not much. You have lunch with Sadie and some young woman named Alexandra Pickering wants to see you at eleven. Says you met her at the Purist house."

"Yes. The Vice President of Events for the Purists. I'm surprised. We did not part on cordial terms."

Nonetheless, Alexandra showed up at precisely eleven. I had to hand it to her, she managed to float on four-inch heels better than any other woman I knew, and her skirts must have been specially made of that swingy knit fabric that makes you look like you're sailing over the floor. She entered with a smile pasted on her face and an invitation in her hand.

"This is for you, Dean Solaris," she said, extending two elegantly manicured fingers holding an envelope. "We thought you might want to sit in the front section of the tent tonight. That way it will be easier for you to connect with Leader Boerum after she's finished."

Alexandra wore the same smug self-confident smile from our first meeting. I marveled at the smoothness of her hair. It was windy outside.

"Thank you, but I may be a bit late to the speech tonight. I have another engagement earlier, so I wouldn't want to intrude on the front section."

"Oh, no problem. I'll save you a seat on the end of the first row, so you can come in anytime without disturbing anyone. But Speaker Boerum specifically said she wanted to see you again."

Now my curiosity was piqued. Why would Danica Boerum give a damn about a university dean?

Alexandra read my thought. "She believes you share an affection for freedom of speech."

"Indeed."

Alexandra turned, actually pirouetted, on her heel. "See you tonight."

Chapter 20

Sadie looked up from her book. "Ah, my favorite mother-to-be." Then, in a move I had not seen before, she was on her feet and hugging me in the middle of Gormley's at lunch hour. Of late, my usually reserved friends seemed to think I needed more physical affection. Behind the crowd at the bar, Wilson McCarthy waved a greeting.

"I've missed you," I said, hugging her back.

"We had dinner together just the other night."

"I know, but I still missed you. So much has happened."

I ordered a cheeseburger from Wilson. My appetite had returned full force since I had seen Joe, alive and uninjured.

"It must have been both frightening and reassuring to see him again in such circumstances," Sadie's lined face was filled with sympathy. "Regrettably, no chance to tell him news of the baby."

"Not yet. But I am feeling better about the whole thing. My state of mind has improved since I saw Joe in person. At least I know where he is and that he's healthy."

"Yes, most reassuring." She smiled. "I wish I could have seen you dressed up like a working girl. That would have made a good photo for your scrapbook." She paused to pour herself more tea. "And I do want to know more about this Veronica. I'm thinking of writing a short story about the sex trade and she might be a perfect character."

I chewed aggressively on the cheeseburger. "She would be, but Veronica's a pretty private person. I doubt she would let you interview her."

"I'm still amazed at the adventure she took you on. But speaking of strange and unbelievable women, are you braced for Danica Boerum's appearance this evening?"

"I've been so busy looking for Joe, I haven't had time for the latest campus news. Have you heard any rumblings about trouble?"

"Oh yes. But nowhere near the outrage I expected. I think many of our students today are much too absorbed in their own lives to work up a head of steam over politics. That's not to say I have stopped worrying about what might happen this evening."

"Are you going?"

"I was thinking about it, but Wilson has gotten very protective of me lately and he's not sure we should attend."

"It could get rough."

"That's what he says."

"Glad to hear the two of you are still an item." I smiled at Sadie, who tilted her head and gave me roguish grin.

"Indeed. As I said, I think this relationship may soon rival you and Joe for romance of the year."

"Not really. Wynan and Nell still hold the title for that one."

"Have you picked out a purple dress?"

"Not yet, but I expect I'll have to wear a purple smock."

We lapsed into our familiar conversation about the university and the usual faculty gossip. Fortunately, my faculty was relatively peaceful this year, so my dependence on Sadie's good advice was less.

"No shootings in the parking lot?" Sadie never let me forget that one of my faculty had shot the other last fall.

"It's early in the academic year."

"Have you filled the vacant spots?"

"I have. Two good young teachers."

"Astonishing how things work out."

"No, what's astonishing is how one crisis replaces another. Now I have to worry about Rosie's attacker and potential violence at tonight's speech."

Tulips had started to bloom in a bed next to the path back to the school of journalism. The mild Nevada winter had not dimmed their vigor, and I smiled at the bright heads as I sat on a bench. I needed a breather before my drive to Reno, and I wanted to consider exactly how I was going to tell Joe about the pregnancy.

My mind went to an evening in January. It had been a dry winter until that night, but then the snow arrived, thick and soft around my house. Joe and I lit a fire and I opened a particularly good bottle of Cabernet.

"I've been saving this for a special occasion, and I think the first snow of the year qualifies."

"Every day with you is a special occasion," Joe had said, and it startled me. My rugged detective lover liked to recite other people's poetry but was not given to expressing sentiments of his own.

"Thank you."

"No, thank you for inviting me into your life, not to mention your home."

"Our home now. Remember, your old apartment was too small for both of us."

We were sitting close on the couch and he leaned back and his hand went to my hair.

"Not just my apartment. My life was too small," he said, staring into the fire. "But you expanded it. Not only with your love but with your reasoning. You've helped me get past the sadness I felt after my parents died and the anger when my best friend killed himself."

"I thought Charlie died in an accident. His death wasn't a suicide."

"I know. And I think I've come to see that now. He was a great guy who drank and drove anyway, and then he died." Joe turned to me. "And I'm glad we named your dog after him."

"Our dog." Charlie snoozed quietly on the hearthrug in front of the fire.

Joe loosened the clip that held back my hair and buried his face in it. Then his head moved down and his lips covered mine. His hand moved under my skirt and began a gentle stroking against my thigh.

"I never thought I could love like this," he said, his breath warm on my neck.

I raised his head and traced the lines around his mouth with my fingers. "I never thought I could either."

Looking back, I reckoned that must have been the night we had conceived the child. Urgency had overtaken us and later, lying together on the couch, we both felt an unusual peacefulness, a bliss that lasted until the next morning.

My doctor was mistaken. I hadn't forgotten birth control. Biology had trumped chemistry.

Wynan and I left for Reno late that afternoon. For the first time since Joe had gone undercover, I remembered why I usually enjoyed going to Reno. As we drove past the ranches that separated Landry from its more famous neighbor, I remembered spending days at the Artown festival that overtakes the city in the summer. Joe and I had walked for hours along the Truckee River that cuts through downtown, listening to the music coming from the park and stopping to watch a dance group practicing for a later session. We had bought our first piece of art together, a delicate watercolor by a local painter we found at an outdoor exhibit.

A sudden stop brought me back to the reality of my mission. We were in the middle of downtown and the pedestrian traffic from the hotel casinos was active.

I patted Wynan's strong hand on the steering wheel. "Thank you for coming with me. I know you think it's stupid and Joe's going to be angry with you for aiding and abetting me twice now."

His handsome face flirted with a smile. "In for a penny, in for a pound. Besides, I'd like to see how this story ends too."

"Did Nell persuade you that I would be all right doing this?"

"Nell told me you were the strongest woman she ever knew, that you had taken defense courses and how effectively you worked with Joe on the previous cases. Of course, I knew that from the time you helped save my granddaughter. But by the time Nell had finished lecturing me about what a heroine you are, I was convinced I wanted to see this adventure through."

"And you wanted to keep me safe."

"And I wanted to keep you safe."

A little past four thirty in the afternoon, we arrived at the neighborhood where Simon lived. Wynan circled the block around Big Al's house, checking to see the locations where he expected the police would be when the raid began.

"You didn't tell the Reno Chief we were coming, did you?"

Wynan gave me a condescending look. "No ma'am, I most certainly did not. And if we stay far enough away, neither the Reno PD nor anyone in Big Al's crew will ever know we were here."

He parked in front of a vacant lot under one of the rare

trees that grew through the sidewalk across the street. We were far enough away from Big Al's house to go unnoticed but close enough to keep an eye on whatever happened. I sat in the backseat wearing dark glasses. My red hair was concealed under a boy's cap and a video game was on my lap braced on a backpack. Wynan wore a baseball cap with the visor low on his face. He leaned back in his driver's seat. Anyone passing by might think he was napping. I was supposed to be a teenager, sitting in back playing a game. One might think both of us were waiting for someone.

At five fifteen, a black van drove into Big Al's driveway and disappeared behind the house. "Heads up." Wynan focused on the house and I leaned forward.

Ten minutes later, a car moved slowly down the street. I could see four men in the car, all in dark windbreakers. The car stopped two houses away from Big Al's and the four men got out. Two were carrying automatic weapons and the others checked their handguns as they moved. The four split up. Two went up to the porch of the house next door to Al's and were admitted by someone I could not see.

"Those two are going to try to get to the back of Al's house," said Wynan, anticipating my question. That would mean climbing over the six-foot-high chain-link fence that separated Al's House from his neighbor. I silently wished them luck.

The other two approached the front of Al's house, but stayed hidden behind a dumpster in front of the house.

"I don't remember that dumpster being there last night," I whispered.

"Probably a gift from Reno PD earlier today," my companion whispered back.

By five thirty, the light was staring to fade. In March the sun still set early. Duskiness fell on the dirty street. I strained to keep my eyes on the two men behind the dumpster.

They emerged, crouching low and moving quickly along the side of Al's house, their heads just below the front windows. As they neared the door a shot rang, followed by a series of shots flashing from an upstairs window.

"Shit, they've been spotted."

The lead man took the porch in one leap and flattened himself against the wall next to the door. The sound of an automatic came from the back of the house. The other two officers must have made it into the backyard.

"Hang in there, Red. This could get messy."

"It's not just Joe. There are children in that house."

"The police know that."

My hands were sweating and I realized I was shaking. My imagination was going crazy. I could envision Joe lying on the floor of that dirty house while Big Al and the others fired at the police. The flashing stopped in the upstairs window but the sound of shooting continued. The fight had moved to the back of the house. The man who was flattened next to the front door motioned to his partner, who sped up and joined him on the other side of the front door. The partner shot at the lock and kicked at the door. Then the door sprung open and both of them disappeared into the house.

Chapter 21

We sat in a silence broken only by the sound of our breathing. Minutes passed. It was unendurable. I strained against the car window. After a few minutes a light went on in one of the downstairs rooms in Big Al's house.

"What's happening?"

"I don't know," whispered Wynan.

"Are any of the cops dead?"

"I don't know. Stop talking."

A patrol car moved in front of the house, red and blue lights flashing. Two uniformed policemen, guns drawn, made their way across the parking area, crouching low. Another patrol car swung in behind the first. Two more uniforms ran toward the house.

One gun shot from inside the house. A shout.

A man appeared in the open door and motioned the uniformed police into the house.

The sound of a girl screaming pierced the air and sent chills through me.

It was almost dark, but the patrol car headlights illuminated the concrete parking area in front of the house. A uniformed policeman emerged and stood on the porch, talking on his phone.

"I think the police are in control," said Wynan, reaching back and putting his hand over mine.

"But we still don't know if anyone's been killed."

"We'll know soon enough. Be brave, sweetheart, be brave." His tone reminded me of Joe. The cap on my head became too much for me and I wrenched it off and used it to blot the tears that were starting to flood my eyes.

An ambulance and a large dark police van moved down the block and parked, blocking off the street to any other traffic. Two uniformed officers emerged from the house. A man, obviously in handcuffs, staggered between them as they headed toward the van. The man was stocky and dark. Not Joe.

The paramedics from the ambulance stopped, spoke briefly to the police and then hastened into the house.

I could barely breathe.

Two more handcuffed men came out with police guiding them to the van. One struggled and fell to his knees, only to be yanked up again and dragged to the van. None of the handcuffed men resembled Big Al or Joe.

"Where's Joe?"

"Be patient."

The paramedics ran out and went to the ambulance. A moment later they wheeled a gurney up the concrete space and through the door. We could hear the sound of men talking in loud voices but the screaming had stopped.

The paramedics wheeled the gurney out. A figure was strapped to the bed. Long hair, small body.

"Too small to be Joe," said Wynan, "Probably one of the girls."

My hand found the handle and I opened the back door. My foot was on the pavement when Wynan's hand gripped my arm. "Back in the car, Red. That was our deal."

I tugged at his grip. "I'm going in. Joe's still in that house. He could be hurt."

Wynan was stronger than I realized. With one pull he had

me back in the car and the door slammed shut. Then he locked the car doors. He turned around to face me. His voice was iron. "You can't do this. If you go in there you'll blow Joe's cover. Some of these pimps are likely to post bail and if they think Joe tipped off the cops, when they get out they'll come after him and kill him for sure."

I slumped back into the car seat. "I'm sorry," was all I could manage. "You're right," I gasped through my heavy breathing.

"And cut out the hyperventilating." His voice was still cold. "You wanted to do this, remember."

Courage, my father's voice said in my head. *Courage. You can handle anything.* Nell had promised Wynan I could do this.

"I'm sorry, Wynan. I promise I'll get hold of myself." My heavy breathing was replaced with a stone in my ribcage. Joe might be dead. I had to face that.

The whoop of the ambulance startled me and I watched it pull away, sirens screeching. Another dark van pulled in to replace it.

Three of the police emerged, herding what looked like a dozen girls toward the new van. The girls, dressed in shorts and flimsy blouses, staggered in high heels and kept their hands pressed to their sides. They walked in a ragged line, some upright and looking straight ahead, others with heads down. One tiny girl who could have been no more than four foot five brought up the rear. She was crying, her face upturned and her mouth open. It was hard to be sure, but I guessed her to be about eleven years old.

Behind the girls came another policeman with a man in handcuffs. The man's face turned toward the light.

Joe. Thick hair rumpled, satin shirt torn at the shoulder.

A thin girl with white-blond hair walked out. She was shown to the backseat of a patrol car while Joe was hustled into the van that held the other men.

Joe and Snowbird.

I sank back into the backseat. I was able to breathe normally again. "Thank God he's okay. And so is Rosie's cousin. Let's go. I've seen enough."

Wynan started the car and slowly moved backward until he turned out into another street.

A cup of hot tea at a delicatessen revived me and relieved Wynan's worries about my health.

"I can't tell you how sorry I am about freaking out in the car," I said.

His fine features relaxed into a grin. Wynan had the sort of good nature that let him forgive easily. No wonder Nell was thrilled to marry him.

"You're in love, babe. I get that. But I couldn't let you out of the car."

"I know. I'm just sorry I panicked. I mean, this was my idea, not yours."

"Right. Ready to go home now?"

"No chance of seeing Joe?"

"No, Joe has to go through the same routines as all the other men in that gang and, sorry to say, may have to spend the night in a cell. But we still have another problem, I think."

"What's that?"

"I didn't see the cops arrest anyone who looked like your description of Big Al. He may have been somewhere else or maybe slipped away. So Reno PD has to make it look like Joe was one of the gang just to be sure his cover is protected. They'll probably take Joe into an interview room to debrief him and then throw him right back into the cell and keep him locked up with the other men until court opens for arraignments tomorrow."

"And the blond girl? I think she might be Snowbird."

"Locked up too. There's nothing more to do here tonight except congratulate yourself on helping the two of them get out of that shithole."

My cell phone rang just as we hit the highway back to Landry. It was Joe. At last.

"Hi, honey. Sorry I haven't called for a while, but I've been too closely watched the last few days and I only have a few minutes now."

"Where are you?"

"I'm in an interview room at Reno headquarters, but I'll have to leave soon so they can put me back in a cell with the others. The chief here says he wants me to thank you for helping them set up the raid this afternoon. It went well. No police were injured."

I decided to wait until another time to tell him that Wynan and I had witnessed it all. "When are you coming home?"

"Sometime tomorrow, I hope. I have to go through arraignment in the morning with these other thugs just to keep my cover intact."

Tomorrow. Thank heavens. A hot meal and a shower and then he would be at my kitchen table and I could tell him everything.

"Joe, did you get Cathy out? Snowbird?"

"We did, although she was a tough sell. She expected to be locked up with the other girls and still doesn't understand why she's in a separate cell and that she's slated to be rescued and sent to rehab while the other girls are to be sent back to their home countries."

"Rosie warned us she might be stubborn."

"We may need Rosie to come to Reno and talk her into it."

"Rosie's in the hospital."

"What? Why?"

"She was beaten up and shot by a man wearing a ski mask. He left her for dead in the parking lot, but fortunately her wounds were not that serious and she's getting better. But she can't come to Reno to see Cathy."

"Jesus, that's awful. Tell her I'll do everything in my power to persuade Cathy to go into rehab."

Rosie's full story and her theories about Danica would be another news item I'd save to tell Joe tomorrow. "I'll tell her Cathy is safe and we'll take it from there. She'll be thrilled to know that."

"And I'll be thrilled to see my girlfriend again." There was noise in the background. "They're here to take me back to my cell. I love you. See you tomorrow."

It was nearly seven when Wynan dropped me off at my house. I splashed some water on my face, changed my clothes and combed my hair back into a respectable bun.

I was exhausted, but I wanted to give Rosie the good news before another night passed. So I fed Charlie, washed down a piece of toast with a glass of milk and headed straight for the hospital.

The evening air was cool but mild and slightly scented with the trees that were budding around the parking lot. The hospital was brightly lit against the dark blue sky and my tiredness left me as soon as I entered the double doors and walked to the elevator.

I was eager to see Rosie and watch her eyes brighten when I told her that her cousin had been rescued.

Young Officer Donovan was sitting on the chair at the end of the hallway near her door. One leg crossed over the other, he balanced a laptop on his knee. He was engrossed in whatever he was reading on his screen.

"Evening, Officer."

He looked up and smiled. "Evening, Dr. Solaris. Come to see our patient?" He rose and knocked on the door for me.

No answer. "She may be asleep."

"I'll just leave a note on her bedside table," I said, entering the dark room. I switched the bedside lamp on and looked at the lump under the bed coverings. A queasy feeling came over me. I pulled back the covers, revealing two pillows end to end, but no Rosie. "Where is she?"

His face paled. "I don't know. She was right here half an hour ago."

"Did you leave at any time?" I demanded.

"Only to take a call at the nurses' station down the hall." He indicated the station twenty yards away. "But I kept my eyes on this part of the hallway the whole time. I swear."

"Did you look into her room when you came on duty?" I was starting to panic again.

"I peeked in but the room was dark and I thought she was asleep. But honest to God, I was sure I saw her in bed."

"Who was on duty before you?"

"A new guy. He was in uniform and in a hurry to leave, so I didn't think to..." The panic I was feeling transferred to the young policeman's face. "Oh Jesus," he said, reaching to his shoulder to call in to the precinct.

Donovan headed for the end of the hall to check the staircase. I searched the rooms on either side of Rosie's. Both empty. I checked the broom closet nearby. Nothing.

Ten minutes later, Norm O'Hare was thundering down the hall. "How the hell did this happen?" For a moment I thought he was going to smash the younger policeman up against the wall.

The three floor nurses fluttered around us, faces filled with concern. All three claimed to have seen nothing. Then an intern showed up. "About an hour ago, I saw a policeman pushing a girl in a wheelchair toward the elevator," he said. "They were laughing like they were going to a party or something."

Laughing? That didn't sound like kidnapping. More like conspiracy.

"What did the policeman look like?" The intern described a man who bore a close resemblance to the curly-haired young man on Rosie's staff I had spoken to yesterday. The intern frowned. "And he wasn't wearing a sidearm, which I thought was odd."

Norm's eyes squinted. "If we assume the so-called policeman was a friend masquerading as a cop, and that Rosie Jenkins left on her own volition, where might she go?"

We decided to split up. Norm and Donovan, still devastated by his error, would search the student newspaper offices and Rosie's apartment.

I had another idea. It seemed I was definitely going to hear Danica Boerum's speech no matter how tired I was.

Chapter 22

I resisted the impulse to call Wynan and tell him about Rosie. The man had given enough of his time to my missions and deserved a quiet evening at home with Nell. Besides, I was sure I knew where I might find Rosie and her costumed conspirator, and I could do that without help.

Bad enough I still had to get through one more night without Joe Morgan. Now I would have to cap off this terrifying day with a visit to the Purist tent and an evening of racist ravings.

Driving to campus, I began to consider my lifelong convictions about freedom of speech. Was it really fair to defend that freedom even for "the thought we hate?" I had always believed so. But was I out of touch with today's world where anyone could say any dreadful thing on social media and get away with it? Was it time for some restriction, some sense of propriety? Bullying online was already outlawed in several states. Some universities had adopted policies of using trigger warnings in classroom lectures and course syllabi. Was I just way behind the times by defending Danica Boerum's appearance?

Questions still swirled inside my head as I parked in a lot near the Purist house. Another car pulled in beside mine and Manny emerged, dressed in a three-piece suit and looking very distinguished. I was still wearing the clothes I had worn to the hospital.

I walked over to him. "I didn't know there was a dress code for tonight."

"I figured if I have to assert my authority, I should look like I had some."

"I'm impressed."

When Manny smiled his whole face lit up. It was impossible not to be charmed. "Good. I'm glad you're impressed. But right now you look perturbed."

"For the last ten minutes I've been having an argument with myself about the wisdom of letting Boerum speak tonight."

"Great. Where were those ideas a few days ago when I was in a quandary?" He took my arm and we started to walk toward the Purist parking lot. "It's too late for your self-doubts. She goes on in twenty minutes."

"I hate ambivalence. I keep thinking that, by now, I should know my own mind and be able to stick to my original opinions."

Manny gripped my hand on his arm. "Changing your mind, occasionally doubting your own wisdom, is normal for people in management positions. Happens to me all the time, and the further up the ladder you go, the more it will happen to you."

I put my hand over his and matched his stride. "I think I have reached the top of my ladder. I love being Dean of Journalism. I don't want more."

He stopped and turned to face me. "Well, you may be offered more, my dear. Stoddard wants to retire next year and he's asked me to apply for the presidency."

"Great. You'd be wonderful."

"And if I get the job, I'll need a new provost." He paused and stared intently at me.

Oh my God.

"And you'd make a splendid one. So get used to the idea of climbing further, Dr. Solaris. I may need you to help me run this place."

On an ordinary evening I would have rushed home to tell Joe and we would have sat in front of the fireplace discussing the consequences to our lives if I became the university provost.

But there was no Joe at home and no time to evaluate consequences. And sure as hell this was not an ordinary evening.

The tent over the parking lot was little more than a large canvas roof. No walls restricted the movements of those looking for seats or standing on the sidelines. The crowd was neither as large as I had feared nor as small as I had hoped.

A stage had been erected at one end of the lot and microphones stood waiting. I spotted a familiar figure standing off to the right of the stage. Big Al was dressed in a suit with a white shirt and tie, looking more like a corporate executive than an over-decorated pimp. Although I doubted he would have approached me in this setting, especially with Manny by my side, I put my hand up to my face, glad I had pulled my hair into a bun. A minute later I saw Al dart back behind the stage and out of sight.

I called Norm O'Hare and got his voicemail. I left him a message to tell the Reno PD they had another arrest to make. I hoped they would get to the tent in time.

I scanned the crowd looking for a pale girl in a wheelchair. But no luck. I was sure I would find her there because she had been so determined to hear Boerum. My apprehension returned.

I let go of Manny's protective arm and moved to a quieter area on the lawn near the tent to call Norm again. This time he answered.

"Rosie wasn't in her apartment," he said, "and now we're looking around the student newsroom. One disturbing development. There's an email addressed to her open on the computer here."

"What does it say?"

"'Mind your own business. Next time I won't miss.'"

"Did she see it?"

"I guess so, because her reply suggested the sender have sex with himself."

"Oh, God. Norm, I think Rosie's heading here. She was absolutely determined to hear Boerum's speech the last time I talked to her."

"Well, we've searched these offices and she's gone. So I'll see you at the speech."

"I'm just scared whoever attacked her in her apartment is going to be here tonight to finish the job. It's possible it's Big Al Boerum, and I just saw him at the tent. Rosie won't be in a protected hospital room. She'll be out in the open."

"Stay calm, Red. I'm on my way."

I turned back toward the tent, and there she was, coming down the path. The boy pushing her wheelchair had ditched his fake police uniform and was dressed in a sweater and khakis. Rosie was keeping warm in a fleece jacket and a plaid blanket over her legs. Her cheeks were pink but the rest of her looked pale and thin.

I approached them. "You damned idiot. Don't you realize the man who shot you is probably here in the crowd?"

For that I got a bittersweet smile. "Probably. And if I spot him, I'll identify him to the security guards."

A burst of air came out of my mouth. "You told the police he wore a mask."

"He did. But I'm good at analyzing body language and I'm looking around for him." She adjusted her blanket pulling it up to her chest. "Besides, no one's going to attack me in front of all these people. Honestly, Red, I need to see Danica Boerum in person. I need to be sure."

"Then I'm sticking with you and your co-conspirator here. Norm is on his way with that young cop who's in love with you."

The boy behind the chair frowned and maneuvered the chair into the sitting area and aligned it with the last row of seats.

"This isn't close enough," said Rosie, twisting her head toward him. "I need to be up front."

"Great. Right where the assholes can see you plain as day," he said.

"Actually, she might be safer up front," I said. "A lot of campus security will be up near the stage. And I have a seat saved at the end of the first row."

Reluctantly, the boy wheeled Rosie up to the front. Alexandra waved at me and pointed to the empty seat at the end with my name on a small white card. Her eyes fell on Rosie and widened. Then she turned away and resumed her conversation with a blond boy dressed in a suit and tie.

The Purists had blocked off half of the first row and labeled seats for university administrators. I saw Manny's name next to mine and was comforted with the thought of his beefy presence next to me. The next three rows were cordoned off with red, white and blue ribbons to indicate where the faithful would sit. Behind these, twenty rows were open to the audience who had started to file in.

Rosie's companion locked her chair at the end of the row next to me. Looking around for Norm, I recognized several of Joe's team in plainclothes scattered among the crowd standing at the sidelines. I also recognized several of the student leaders I had met with earlier. They and their friends were sitting, hands folded in their laps. One saw me and drew her fingers across her lips to indicate they were zipped shut. Good. I prayed the strategy of silence might work to prevent trouble.

At exactly eight thirty, the blond boy in the suit walked up on the stage and stood in front of the microphone. He snapped his fingers. "This is how we applaud," he said, snapping them again.

The sound of snapping fingers started offstage where the tent roof met the Purist house. The Purists marched out of the house by a side door in single file, snapping their fingers in rhythm. The men wore navy blazers with white shirts and red ties. The women wore long navy skirts with high neck white blouses and red sashes. They paraded single file in lock step like soldiers, marching in front of the stage and then into the specially marked rows of seats.

Backs straight, eyes forward, not a murmur from anyone, they reminded me of a religious cult I had once covered as a reporter.

The blond boy took the microphone again to welcome the audience and introduce Danica Boerum: "one of our great political leaders, fighter for a purer America, defender of our Constitution." He snapped his fingers and the Purists reacted, raising their arms and snapping in unison.

Danica Boerum came onto the stage, emerging from the darkness behind her. Her snow-white hair gleamed under the lights suspended from the tent roof. It was even shorter than her newspaper photos showed, cropped so closely she looked almost mannish with her striking nose and dark eyes. She was dressed in a long white gown with full sleeves and an American flag brooch pinned on her shoulder. She accepted the microphone from the blond boy, unhitched it from its stand and began to pace back and forth across the stage. She said nothing for a full fifteen seconds, then stopped, looked out over the crowd and smiled. Large teeth as white as her hair.

Most of us who were in the audience that night had trouble recalling exactly what Danica said at the beginning. There were no dramatic or sensational phrases, no uniquely quotable comments, although the attending press took copious notes. She employed the standard political calls for a stronger democracy, a return to American greatness, our exceptional history.

When she finally got to her principle call for sending immigrants back to their own countries, she spoke softly and with a smile, conceding the contributions foreigners had made but still insisting that this was not the place for them to call home. Her arguments for white rule were couched in short biographies about famous white men in American and northern European history. Men who mattered, she said, men who governed wisely.

She paused at times to permit someone to signal the Purists who obediently raised their arms and snapped.

To my surprise, the rest of the audience remained quiet. Truly quiet. No outbursts, no shouts from the sidelines. Clearly people had gotten the message about the strategy of silence and had passed it on.

After about twenty minutes, the strategy began to take a toll on the speaker. She raised her voice a notch and projected it past the Purist ranks to the general audience.

"If you don't like snapping your fingers, feel free to applaud," she said. Another smile. "Or boo if you prefer. I can handle criticism."

Silence.

One of the Purist boys raised his hand. "Tell us again why it's so important that the white race be the only ones who govern America."

The smile disappeared. "Members of the other races are good people and have given us wonderful art and music. But their record of governance in their own home countries is disappointing. Their countries are consumed with corruption and violence. Clearly, they are weak as leaders of societies."

Silence.

A Purist girl stood up. "And isn't it true dark-skinned people are responsible for most of the crime in this country?"

Danica nodded. "Most of the violent crime."

The Purists snapped their fingers.

My gag reflex went off. Jesus, I could see where this was going, but I didn't know how to stop it. Obviously the Purists wanted a fight. A fist fight, a knife fight, anything that would get the TV cameras rolling.

Remarkably, the crowd remained silent. Manny took my hand and squeezed it.

Danica made one more try. Her voice rose: "America is our home. Our home. Not theirs. And we must do everything in our power to reclaim it for ourselves. We must defy those who question us and be rid of those who don't belong here. By force if necessary."

The Purists rose as one and raised their arms snapping their fingers. Danica put out her hands and signaled them to sit down. Her eyes flashed with anger. She addressed the crowd at the sidelines. "Surely, someone has a question."

There was a slight stirring among the crowd, but no one spoke.

"I have a question." The voice came from my left side.

Oh shit, I had forgotten to tell Rosie about the silence strategy. The girl had half risen from her wheelchair.

Danica's eyes turned to Rosie.

Rosie's voice was loud and firm. "Miss Boerum, how do you go from a job running whores in Los Angeles to being a spokeswoman for The American Purists?"

Danica's face turned to stone. "I have no idea what you mean."

Rosie shouted, "Oh yes you do. I remember you, Danica. I remember when you weren't Danica. You were Mama D, pimping out twelve-year-olds. I know who you really are." She collapsed back into her wheelchair.

Two bodies came at Rosie from different directions. One was Big Al, moving fast, his hand reaching for something inside his jacket. The other was Norm O'Hare, also moving fast, holding his badge out front.

The two men faced each other over the pale girl. "Get her out of here," said Big Al through clenched teeth.

Norm grabbed the handles of Rosie's chair, spun her around and headed for the exit.

Big Al turned and raced into the darkness behind the stage.

A rumbling sound came from behind me. It was the sound of chairs being moved as people stood. I turned. Members of the still-silent audience were holding up large placards. In bold ink, each carried a different message. "America is for all of us." "Down with racism." "Long live diversity." "We are all brothers and sisters." The entire audience was on its feet, still quiet but pumping the placards up and down. Someone started to sing, "Oh beautiful for spacious skies" in a strong tenor voice. Gradually the whole audience joined in. A trumpet played a riff from somewhere outside on the lawn. The voices grew louder as Manny and I edged back through the crowd still standing and singing. As we came to the lawn outside we could hear "and crown thy good with brotherhood," now so loud I was sure they could hear it in San Francisco.

Manny leaned into my ear. "Your silent strategy may have worked, but I'm glad to see our students still found another way to express themselves."

"I'm glad too." I turned to the students filing out behind us and gave them two thumbs up.

I could still see the stage from the lawn. The blond boy had reached Danica's side. She stood frozen, staring out into the singing crowd. The boy put his hand on her elbow. "Thank you all for coming," he said into the mic, although I doubt anyone in the retreating audience heard. Then he guided the speaker off the stage.

Chapter 23

The singing stopped but the trumpet kept playing "America the Beautiful" somewhere in the night. Then we heard it joined by drums, followed by a sax and a tuba as it became clear that students from all over campus were marching past the Purist tent, many linking arms and some carrying placards. I glanced over at a group of Purists standing in front of their house. They stood dumb and confused. Alexandra Pickering's tears streamed mascara down her cheeks.

Manny took my arm again. "Another great evening in paradise, don't you think?"

I squeezed his arm. "You bet. I'm so proud of our students."

"Gandhi would have been proud. The students figured out how to protest. Their decision to use music instead of fists and guns was genius," he said. "Now tell me, what was that business with Rosie Jenkins all about? She accused Danica of running whores?"

"Rosie told me she thought she knew Danica Boerum from her past. I guess seeing her in person tonight made her certain."

"Wow. That's astonishing. Who's the guy who wheeled her out of there?

"That's Norm O'Hare, a Landry detective investigating the attack on Rosie. My guess is he's taking her back to the hospital."

The students were still marching but now singing and shouting to each other into the open air. Manny and I diverted to a smaller path where it was quieter. He was still shaking his head in disbelief. "If Rosie is right about Danica Boerum, the question she asked is pertinent. How does a woman go from sex trafficker to Purist promoter?"

"That's a mystery yet to be solved. Right now my worry is for Rosie's safety. The other man who headed for her is a known pimp and a vicious guy. I suspect he is also Boerum's brother, given the physical resemblance. He should have been arrested earlier today but he escaped. I've already alerted Norm to this but I should call him again."

Manny left me with a quick hug and moved back toward a cluster of students still marching and pumping their placards. I moved farther down the path to make the call, but Norm's phone went to voicemail. I left a message and decided to get to the hospital as quickly as possible.

At the end of the path near the journalism parking lot, I encountered three male students. Two white students were holding the third, an African-American boy who was shaking with rage, his fists clenched.

"Are you okay?" I asked, looking at the boy in distress.

"I will be," he said, eyes flashing. "You were right, Dean Solaris. I shouldn't have gone to that speech. I wanted to shout out even though we had agreed to be silent. What I really wanted to do was jump up on that stage. More than anything, I wanted to kill that bitch."

"Get in line," said one of his companions. "C'mon, let's get back to the house. You need a stiff drink and so do I." He led the boy away.

The third student lingered behind. I recognized him as a former student of mine, now the head of the inter-fraternity council who attended Manny's meeting. "I'm glad I came," he said. It was then I noticed his eyes were watering. "I knew I was going to despise what Boerum said." He wiped his eyes with the back of his hand. "But I didn't know how much it would hurt."

"Hate speech does hurt."

"The black guy you just spoke to is one of my best friends. I've known him since grade school. We're in the same fraternity. My parents are friends with his parents. But I don't think until now I ever really understood what he's had to put up with all his life."

"You probably still don't. Neither of us does."

I started to walk toward my car but the boy stayed by my side. "It's late, Dean Solaris. I'll see you to your car."

"Thank you. You said you were glad you came to the speech tonight. Why?"

He was breathing heavily. "You said in an ethics class I took from you that the opinion that contradicts our own is valuable, that we should listen to those we disagree with because it will refine our critical thinking."

"And you think that's what happened tonight?"

We had reached the car and I unlocked the door. The student put his hand on the top of the door and looked at me. His eyes were clear now.

"I know it did. I realized tonight that I've been too casual about racism and too indifferent to politics in this country. I always figured that was crap for other people to worry about. I haven't even registered to vote yet. But now I will, because after listening to that woman and the bigotry of those Purist bastards, I know what I have to fight for and fight against. As hard as I can."

Then the boy turned and walked back toward where he had left his friends. I sat in my car for a moment. Maybe I'd been right all along to support Boerum's right to speak. The students had behaved magnificently, and despite the hurt feelings I had just witnessed, perhaps the lesson had outweighed the emotional injury some had experienced.

Maybe. I still wasn't sure. The memory of the boy shaking with rage would stay with me a long time.

The hospital corridor was empty except for the familiar sight of Norm O'Hare pacing in front of Rosie's door. He was on his phone and as I came closer, I heard: "Tell them that we don't have anything to charge Danica Boerum with in Nevada. They'll have to send someone from LA with a warrant." He motioned me toward him. "I'm on the phone with LAPD. Go on in." He inclined his head toward the door of Rosie's room.

Rosie, propped up in her bed, was also on the phone. "I'll see you tomorrow morning. Eight o'clock sharp. And I'm turning the set on now so I can catch you on the news." She grinned wickedly at me. "That was a reporter from the *Los Angeles Times* who was here tonight watching the speech."

"How are you feeling, Rosie?" My voice was dead calm even if my brain was racing.

"I'm feeling grand, Dr. Solaris. How about you?"

"I'm feeling a little terrified, thanks just the same. Do you know who that big man rushing toward you was?"

Wicked smile again. "Yup. That was Big Al. I remember him too. He's Mama D's brother. And I'll bet he's the one who shot me."

I sat on the edge of her bed and took her thin white hand in mine. I wanted to squeeze it hard to get her serious attention, but I settled for a firm hold. "Then you know he's very dangerous, Rosie. And you, my friend, are now in grave danger after that stunt you pulled at the speech."

Rosie squeezed my hand. "It'll be okay, Red. I'm fine. I'm guarded by police day and night, if you hadn't noticed. Besides, you don't know pimps the way I do. They hate the limelight. My bet is Big Al and his sister and their whole crew are headed out of town as fast as they can."

"You made a spectacle of her tonight. I think the Purists are still shaken up by what you said."

"Good. But I doubt it will bring them to their senses. They love their ideas too much. As for Boerum, if what happened tonight gets into the media, she'll give a press conference in a day or two, denounce me as mentally ill, deny everything I said, and move on."

I sighed.

"Except she may get caught this time," Rosie added. "That reporter I was just talking to on the phone has been following Boerum for two or three years trying to get information on her and her group and their headquarters in Idaho. He was there tonight and he also attended campus riots at other places. He's done a lot of research and written two big stories about the Purists for his paper. He's coming to interview me tomorrow morning and he's going to be on the local news tonight."

"I'm not sure it's wise for you to talk to him. It will certainly get the Boerums right back on your case."

"Stop being such a pessimist, Red. This might be big news. Who knows, maybe I can get a job at the *LA Times* after graduation." Rosie was bouncing up and down in her bed.

"Okay, settle down. I'm going to stay with you for a while."

"Great, we can watch the news together."

Norm opened the door. "I put myself on duty here tonight, ladies. So if you need me, I'll be right outside."

"Any luck finding Big Al?"

"Not yet. He dodged my team at the speech but they're looking for him."

* * *

The local news began at ten and Rosie had the set tuned in before the credits came on. The anchor announced a special interview with Jake Barlow of the *Los Angeles Times* on the events of the evening and the story behind Danica's Boerum's rise to prominence.

Jake Barlow turned out to be a slender, rather mousy-looking man with thick glasses, not quite the image of the intrepid reporter Rosie had described. But he spoke with a surprisingly strong voice and seemed to know his stuff when it came to Danica and the Purists.

The interviewer, a thin-faced man with cupid bow lips and a sallow complexion began. "Jake Barlow, you have just come from a remarkable speech given by Danica Boerum on the Mountain West Campus. Perhaps what was most remarkable was the student reaction. Tell us, did they really remain silent throughout and then burst into 'America the Beautiful?'"

"Indeed, they did. Best student protest I've ever seen."

"And this was occasioned by Boerum's speech. Tell us what you know about her."

"Until tonight, all I knew was that Danica Boerum joined the Purists in Idaho about eight years ago," Barlow said. "Apparently she caught the eye of one of the men in the Purist leadership who brought her to Idaho where she became very popular with the rest of the group. My sources tell me she lived with the leader for a few years and then they had some sort of falling out and Danica struck out on her own. She began to speak at Purist events, first extemporaneously and later giving more formal addresses. The Purist faithful were enchanted and after a year or two, she was the primary spokesperson and considered a leader herself."

"You said 'until tonight.' Did the one outspoken student's

accusation lead you to new information? Did Boerum ever mention she was from Los Angeles?"

"It did indeed. None of us have ever been able to persuade Boerum to speak about her past," said Barlow. "If you read the transcripts of her speeches, she's never mentioned anything about her childhood or her parents or any family before the Purists. She refused almost any attempt to interview her unless it was about her speeches. And when I tried to get any information about her personal life or her past, I got cut off. The Purists were quite threatening whenever someone from the press approached her on the wrong subject."

"So how did you get information for the articles you wrote?"

"I interviewed several ex-members of the Idaho Purist group and then followed up with some former disciples in southern Nevada. I learned a great deal about their beliefs in nativism and American exceptionalism."

"Are they gun owners who practice any kind of guerilla warfare?"

"No, they leave the military stuff to other white separatist groups. But the Purists do admit they are perfectly happy to provoke violence whenever they stage an event like tonight's. They do believe that the violence is what gets them the media coverage they need to recruit new members."

"Like the jihadists?"

"They seem more interested in martyrdom than action. They see provocation as a way to draw violence upon themselves. As one guy in Vegas said to me, 'Purists always want to be seen as the clean, law-abiding white folks who are being attacked by the minorities. That's what recruits new members to their cause."

"So tell us what you learned about Danica Boerum's past tonight and the girl who made that accusation."

"Until tonight, I had never gotten a specific lead on Danica

Boerum's life before the Purists, where she came from, and certainly no indication she had ever trafficked kids in LA."

"Are you sure the female student who spoke out at the rally tonight is telling the truth?"

"I talked to her on the phone and I'm seeing the girl tomorrow. But what she said fits."

"How so?" The interviewer looked perplexed. "It strikes me as odd that a woman who promotes her brand of political discourse and who plays a leadership role in a group who calls themselves pure would have ever come from a background as a prostitute or a pimp."

Barlow took a sip of water and nodded his head. "Maybe. But it's not as odd as you think. After about twenty minutes on the phone with the student who said she knew Boerum in Los Angeles, I called my contacts in the Los Angeles Police Department and asked them about a Mama D. I learned that they had quite a file on a female trafficker named Mama D who ran young girls a decade ago and then disappeared. They never knew her real name and were never able to indict her for anything, but she was arrested once and they do have a mug shot of Mama D from eight years ago."

The screen changed to a black and white photo of a fierce-looking woman with long black hair. The face was younger, but definitely Danica Boerum.

"That's her. That's when she was in the life," Rosie pounded her pillow. "I knew it."

"But I still don't get the motive for her transition," said the anchor.

"Years ago, the LAPD was getting evidence on Mama D's activities and closing in," said Barlow. "Tonight, one of my police sources told me Mama D left California in a hurry, a few steps ahead of the authorities. Now we know that the guy from Idaho provided her a way out and a new way to make money. So she moved up north, and two years later she had renewed her old driver's license, resumed her birth name of Danica Boerum and transformed into a radical politician. The Purists raise some hefty sums from their supporters and Boerum lives well on what they pay her for speaking."

"It's still hard to believe," said the anchor. "I mean, the police had her picture and she's often been photographed in the press."

"With markedly changed hair," said Barlow. "Women who sell sex know quite a bit about transformation and pretense. Boerum was smart enough to realize that she didn't have to undergo plastic surgery to disguise herself. All she needed was a new life and a very different persona to get the police off her trail. And it worked. I can assure you that until I called them tonight with my story, the LAPD never connected the dots on this one."

"But I did. I did," said Rosie, bouncing again.

"You're going to rip out your stitches, young lady."

"So what happens now?" asked the anchor.

"Well, we're in legal limbo for a while. Nevada won't charge her because she's committed no crime in this state. So California will have to try to extradite her to get her back. The real question will be if the statute of limitations will protect her from extradition."

"I don't believe this," said Rosie, sinking back into her pillows.

The anchor leaned forward toward Barlow. "But surely this story and this news about her past will affect her reputation."

"One would think so. I imagine the Purists are scrambling right now. Probably to find ways to deny the accusation and protect their spokeswoman."

"But you found the student credible?"

"Yes. Along with the photo of Mama D. But I'll know much

more tomorrow when I interview the student who accused her. And LAPD is sending a detective who knew Mama D up here tomorrow to interview the student as well. Maybe a case can be put together."

"Fascinating if the student's story turns out to be true."

"Dammit. It is true," moaned Rosie.

"Settle down," I said as the TV screen faded to black and went into a commercial. "You'll have your chance tomorrow to give Barlow the full story and to give the LAPD whatever help you can so they can go after Boerum."

Another moan of protest.

I went to her bed and adjusted her pillows. "Meanwhile, you need to get some sleep. You're exhausted and your wounds are still healing."

Chapter 24

It took another hour to persuade Rosie to stop talking and get some sleep. Her excitement was infectious and I was truly proud of her. I decided to stay in her room for at least part of the night and suggested to Norm that he might want to beef up the police presence in the hospital. I was less convinced than Rosie that the Boerums were headed out of town. And since the interview with Barlow, I was sure she'd be seen as a target for renewed effort by her attacker, now likelier than ever to be Big Al.

Norm was way ahead of me and had already posted extra guards at the hospital entrances. He had also alerted the Reno police to Big Al's whereabouts. Maybe they could catch that son of a bitch before he tried to do more harm.

Knowing that I couldn't see Joe until the next day, the prospect of another night in my lonely bed did not appeal as much as helping protect Rosie.

I must have dozed off in my chair, because the noise that woke me at two in the morning was so subtle that at first I thought it was part of a dream. But somehow my internal alarm system went off and I decided to check it out. My body was stiff from sleeping in the chair and I was still stretching when I noticed the door handle move. I froze in place and then looked around for something to use as a weapon in case the person opening the door was not police. Rosie's wheelchair was near the door, but no other hard object was in sight. I stepped over to the chair, grasped the handles and pulled it back toward me.

The door opened slowly, letting in light from the hall. A man taller than Norm or Donovan was silhouetted against the light.

"Who are you?"

The figure continued to move toward me. It was a man. Tall and bulky. "Be very quiet," came a whispered command.

"Who the hell are you?" I said in a louder voice. But I knew who it was, and my blood ran cold.

The figure stepped closer and I shoved the wheelchair against his legs.

"Shit."

The light flicked on over Rosie's bed. She was sitting and staring wide eyed. Big Al leaned over and grabbed the armrests of the wheelchair and pushed with all his might. I dodged most of it but part of the wheel caught my shin as it crashed past me and hit the wall.

"Well, if it isn't Patty Cake." The most terrifying smile I'd ever seen spread across his face. He crossed the room in one long step and grabbed both my arms. "What a surprise to see you here."

Rosie reached for her phone. Al whirled around, and with one swipe, flung the phone across the room. "You take care of the kid," he said to someone behind him in the hallway. "I've got this one." He dug his fingers into my armpits, grasped my shoulders and dragged me to the door.

I screamed and pummeled him with my fists, but it did no good. I let my legs go limp to try to slow him down, but he shook me and dug his fingernails farther into my arms and pulled again until I was out in the hall.

I could hear Rosie screaming for help behind me.

Someone dressed in white moved past us and into the room. "Shut up," I heard her say, and she slammed the door shut.

Big Al dragged me farther out into the hall, past the body of Norm O'Hare lying on the floor next to the chair. A knife protruded from Norm's neck and his eyes were open and dead. It was clear the knife had severed the carotid artery. Blood pooled around Norm's head and shoulders and made the hallway slippery. I straightened out my leg and tried to gain some stance against Al, but my foot slipped in the blood and I half fell to the floor.

Al pulled me up again and pushed me down the hall away from Rosie's room. I shouted for help to the empty hallway. Al held me with one hand tight around my arm and slapped me hard across the face with the other.

"Shut up, bitch." He opened another door to the cleaning closet I had searched before and pushed me inside. I staggered and fell to my knees. His hand came across my face in another slap so hard I almost lost consciousness. "You owe me, Patty Cake, and I'm gonna collect right now."

He took off his jacket and unbuckled his belt.

My head cleared enough to see brooms and mops stacked against the back of the closet and shelves with bottles and rags. A single bulb burned in the ceiling. A bottle of cleaning fluid was on the shelf closest to me. I grabbed at the bottle and swung for his face. But he was too fast and his hand shot up, smashing the bottle to the floor.

Before I could look for another weapon his arms were around me and he forced me down on the floor.

I knew I should fight back. Al was sure to kill me after he'd gotten what he wanted. My mind struggled to remember what I had learned from my self-defense lessons. One thing I knew was I should have started fighting back when we were still in Rosie's room. I had waited too long and now I was on the floor with a monster intent on rape and murder.

The closet smelled of dust and disinfectant and the

linoleum was slippery. It was hard to get any purchase with my leather shoes against the floor. I lifted one knee and Al's fist came back and pounded it down. His weight was full on me and I tried to twist away, but couldn't. Then he lifted up and took one hand off my left shoulder to unzip his pants. I twisted again, freeing up one of my arms.

The elbow is stronger than you realize, my instructor had said. I aimed my elbow and struck his nose as hard as I could.

He roared and used his hand to cup his bleeding nose. I twisted farther and thrust my hip to throw him off balance. He fell to the side, used his other hand to balance against the floor and in the process freed my right shoulder. I pulled my legs out from under him and aimed a hard kick at his knee. He roared again and bent backward, transferring his hand from his bleeding nose to his leg. I kicked again, this time aiming for just under the ribcage and hoping to strike at his solar plexus. I missed and he stood up, preparing to attack again. But his loosened pants fell to his knees and caused him to stagger. That gave me time to get to my feet and aim my kick again, this time for his unprotected groin. He collapsed on the floor.

Grabbing an upper shelf, I steadied myself in a standing position, shook my head to clear the pain and delivered two more kicks. One to the head and another to the solar plexus. He moaned but lay still on the floor.

I lifted my foot and brought the heel of my shoe down hard above his ear directly on the temple of his forehead. That silenced him. He was unconscious. If I had been accurate, maybe he was out forever.

I grabbed a broom handle, pushed Al's legs aside and opened the door into the hallway. Norm's body was still there and the door to Rosie's room was closed but I could hear a voice behind it. "You retract every fucking word you said tonight or the next bullet I fire at you is going into your miniscule brain."

I edged past Norm's body and put my hand on the handle of the door to Rosie's room.

"You're finished, Mama D. And you know it."

I flung open the door and saw Rosie on her knees in the center of her bed, her fists clenched, a harsh fluorescent light from the overhead fixture spilling over her pale face.

Danica Boerum leaned against the wall. She was still wearing the long white dress she had appeared in at her speech. A black revolver was in her right hand, aimed at Rosie.

I was still breathing hard as she turned toward me and turned the gun, aiming at my chest. Out of the corner of my eye, I saw Rosie jump from the bed and leap toward Danica. One pale thin arm came up under Danica's hand. The gun roared and I felt a sharp stabbing in my right arm. I staggered back against the wall, holding my upper arm as blood ran through my fingers.

Danica wheeled toward Rosie and raised her arm to bring the barrel of the gun down. She struck Rosie full on the face. Rosie sank back onto the bed, her cheek a mass of blood.

Danica stood upright and spoke in her calm professional voice. "Listen carefully. You're going to retract everything you said tonight. When that reporter shows up tomorrow you're going to tell him that you were mistaken. Seriously mistaken. And then you're going to offer a public apology."

Rosie moaned and spit out some blood, but her eyes remained defiant. "Or what, Mama D?"

Danica looked over at me. I was now hunched against the wall, holding my right arm and trying to put pressure on the gunshot wound.

"Or I'm going kill your friend here."

Rosie was back up on her knees. "Oh yeah. And when they find the Dean of Journalism lying dead in my room, you don't suppose there will be any questions asked?"

Danica stared at me. She recognized me, and it was clear she was measuring alternatives. Then she turned back to Rosie. Her voice rose. "Okay, bitch. Here's how it will play out. Al and I will take this lady with us and keep her in a safe place while you retract your statement to that reporter. Same for whatever you say to the LAPD. If you want your dean to come back alive, you'll tell everyone you made a serious mistake."

Danica didn't know that Al was out of commission in a broom closet down the hall. And she hadn't stopped long enough to wonder how I got away from him.

Danica took a step toward Rosie. "Then tomorrow morning when you tell that reporter from the *Times* that you made it all up," Danica reached for the tissue box next to Rosie's bed, "you're going to say you got that cut on your cheek from an unknown intruder, whoever killed the cop outside in the hall." She tossed the box on the bed. "Here, wipe your face."

Rosie spit more blood. "Why would I say any of that?"

Danica cocked her head toward me. "Because if you don't, then tomorrow morning will be the last morning your friendly dean will ever see."

Rosie slumped.

Danica moved toward me. I lunged for her gun hand, but she was too fast for me and dodged to the door. With one hand on the door handle, she opened the door a few inches. She aimed the gun at my belly and I instinctively put my hands over it. She waved the gun slightly. "Come quietly, Dean Solaris. Unless you want another gunshot wound." She stuck her head out the door. "Al, come here."

"If you take her, I'll tell that reporter everything," shouted Rosie, now standing beside her bed. "I'll tell him how you pimped out twelve-year-olds and how you beat up the girls who disobeyed you or tried to run away. I'll give him names and dates and street corners." Rosie wiped the blood from her mouth. "And I'll tell the cops everything too. You brought girls across state lines, so that will bring the feds in, Mama D. You'll have no place to run to anywhere in this country. You're cooked, lady. You're all over." Rosie was breathless by the time she finished, but Danica seemed unmoved by her threat. She waved the gun at me again and motioned for me to come to the door.

Danica called again out of the open doorway. "Al, come here. I need you." She waited a moment and then called out again, "Al, get your ass in here."

A frown appeared on her face.

I made another decision. "Al's not going to be much help tonight," I said. "You're going to have to deal with both of us on your own."

Danica waved the gun from me to Rosie and then back again. Her eyes were full of hatred and then fear. "What happened to Al?"

"I happened to Al." My voice was hoarse.

"Is he dead?"

"I sure as hell hope so."

She paused, then stepped back and raised the gun up with both hands. The barrel was pointed directly at my forehead. Danica was about to fire again when a dark figure appeared in the doorway behind her and grabbed her wrist. Another shot rang out and shattered the overhead light. The room fell into darkness except for the light over Rosie's bed. I could hear the sounds of a struggle but my eyes could not make out the dark figure.

Through the dimness I heard, "God damn you, let me go." I heard the voice of the dark figure say something but I couldn't make out the words. The pain in my shoulder became more intense and overwhelmed me. The room began to fade as I passed out.

Chapter 25

A brilliant white light shown above my head, and far in the distance, a man's voice said, "You're in surgery, Dr. Solaris. Now, please count backwards from 100..."

I obeyed. "99, 98, 97..." The baby? Oh God. Did anyone tell them I was pregnant?

"Keep counting."

"96, 95..."

Orange leaves, everywhere, floating in front of me. I sat under a brilliant maple tree at the far end of a courtyard. In the distance I saw people dancing. Some were clustered around Nell, who was wearing a silk brocade suit that matched her curly hair. Wynan stood beside her in a tuxedo. I put my hand on my belly. It was enormous under a dark purple maternity dress.

The wedding must have happened.

I looked again at Nell and the dancing people. They were walking off the dance floor, following Nell and Wynan down a hill toward a lake in the distance. A photographer led the way. Why wasn't I with them if I had been in the wedding?

"That should have been you down there by the lake." Evangeline sat down beside me and sipped from a glass of Champagne. "You should have had one of these for yourself," she said.

"Champagne?"

An ironic smile. "No. A wedding." Then her face became sad and she looked older than when I had seen her in Sacramento.

"It didn't work out," I said but did not know why.

"I know. That's why I'm here. I took a leave," she said, twirling her empty glass. "You'll need someone here for the first few weeks."

The orange leaves began to swirl around me, blocking out the scene. Then they fell to the ground in a great heap over my feet. I looked up at Evangeline. But she was gone. The leaves blew up again swirling madly, a sea of orange. Then nothing. I was alone.

"Meredith," I heard a woman's voice whisper behind me. I turned but no one was there.

"I think she's coming round," said the voice.

"Red. Honey."

I opened my eyes and found myself staring into the face of a man who needed a shave, and judging by the redness around his eyes, had not slept in a long while.

He leaned over me and bent down to kiss me gently. I could feel the sharp stubble on his chin brush across my lips.

"I gather she's more to you than just a witness," said the woman's voice.

He sat back and a nurse appeared from behind my bed and took my wrist in her hand to read my pulse. I looked up at her. "How long have I been out?"

"About twelve hours," she answered, still looking at her watch. She was the same nurse who had attended Rosie, the woman with the round face and the old-fashioned braid circling her head. Her touch was soft and she had kind blue eyes. She injected something into the tube that ran into my arm. "This will help the pain," she said.

"What time is it now?" My voice sounded raw.

"Nearly noon," she said.

I cocked my head toward the man. "How long has he been here?"

She smiled. "Since early morning, I would say. This nice detective hasn't left your side for so much as a cup of coffee."

I turned to the man. "Good to see you, mister. I've missed your face."

A smile cracked through the stubble around his mouth. He took my other hand and raised it to his lips. "You had me scared for a while there."

"Are you home for good?"

"I am." A light went on in his dark green eyes with a look of such tenderness it made my throat close.

"God, I missed you," we said simultaneously.

Joe reached in and stroked my cheek. "I gather you've been taking risks again." His voice was gentle without a hint of disapproval.

"What happened? I remember Danica Boerum with a gun threatening Rosie. She shot me in the arm and then I went blank."

"The doctor says the bullet went through the fleshy part but missed the bone," he said.

"Your arm will be sore for a while, but you should make a decent recovery," said the nurse, walking to the door. "I'll tell the doctor you're awake."

A terrible cloud passed over my mind. The image of a pale girl with blood all over one side of her face. "Rosie? What happened to her?"

Joe leaned forward and took my hand again. "Rosie's okay. She'll have a badly bruised face for a while, but no bones were broken. She's devastated about what happened."

"And Danica?"

"In the Landry jail, waiting for the feds to come and take her to federal prison."

"Did you stop her? I remember someone coming in while she was aiming that gun at my head."

"No. That was a young patrolman who I guess Norm had assigned to the room. Something Donovan. I didn't get here until it was all over."

"Norm?"

The light went out of Joe's eyes. "Gone. Rosie still hasn't stopped crying for him."

I remembered the stocky figure barreling down the hall dragging the young patrolman who fell for Rosie and had probably saved our lives.

"Norm stayed here last night because he wanted to protect us."

"And if Big Al recovers from the beating he took, he and his sister will be tried for the murder of my good friend, Norman O'Hare."

I remembered that last moment in the closet when I had brought the heel of my shoe down on Al's temple. I was wearing leather flats with an inch heel, sharp around the edges and hard as steel. I had hoped to end big Al with that move. "How bad is he?"

"Serious brain damage." Joe leaned back in his chair and regarded me with his cop face, unsmiling and a little intimidating. "That was your work, wasn't it?"

"It was. And at the time, I hoped I had killed him. He dragged me past Norm's body and through Norm's blood to get into that closet."

Joe shook his head as if to get rid of the image. Then the green eyes came back to me. "The police on the case said you were shot and bruised but there was no evidence of rape, even though Al's pants were down around his knees."

I let out a long breath. "He never got that far. That self-defense course you insisted I take finally paid off."

Another tiny smile played around the stubbled mouth. This one was bittersweet. "I should have known that bastard would come looking for you when he got away from the police raid at his house."

"Did you know he was Danica Boerum's brother?"

"Until this morning, all I knew about Al Boerum was that he was the chief thug who hired me to drive his underage girls up to Reno." Joe ran his thumb across his chin. "But I did know he was interested in you, because all he could talk about after you saw me was the hot redhead who owed him one."

"And Danica is going to federal prison? Why federal?"

"She took girls across state lines. It even appears she took some by force back in the old days. So there's been a federal warrant on her for some time. She should do a lot of time. Particularly if there's any evidence she helped her brother kill Norm. They're checking the knife for prints. His and hers."

The pain in my arm throbbed and I began to wonder what other injuries I had sustained. Instinctively my good arm and hand went to my belly. "Did any other part of me get hurt?"

Joe's face came closer to mine. "Sweetheart, a gunshot wound is serious enough. As far as I've been told, the rest of you is bruised but okay."

I shuddered and changed the subject. "How's Rosie's cousin?"

Joe took my hand. "I think she'll be all right. Snowbird is Cathy again. It took me and a counselor most of last night to convince her to go to that rehab home in Colorado. Then I ordered in some strawberry ice cream and she began to take me seriously. I told her Rosie had sent me after her, that Rosie was in the hospital and she was determined Cathy had to be rescued. She finally agreed."

"Strawberry with sprinkles?"

"You got it."

"Great. Do you still have to be arraigned?"

"No, thank God. After he learned what happened here, Wynan drove to Reno at the crack of dawn and got me released. The Reno squad thanked me and gave us a police escort. We must have been doing ninety on the highway."

"I'm so glad you're here."

"So am I, sweetheart."

"There's something else we have to talk about."

The door opened and a familiar face appeared and came to the foot of my bed, engrossed in the chart she carried. Dr. Helen Ferguson came around to my side, looked briefly at the bandaged arm and then put her stethoscope to my chest.

"Joe, this is my regular doctor, Helen Ferguson. Helen, this is Joe Morgan."

"Your beloved?" she asked, looking at Joe's tired face without letting go of the stethoscope.

"Yes." I felt an unusual blush as she ran the scope down to my belly.

"The docs here say you're going to be fine, just a flesh wound to that shoulder. Rest of you seems good. The fetal heartbeat sounds strong," she said.

Joe's eyes narrowed. "Fetal heartbeat?"

"Joe just got back from a mission, Helen. He's a detective and was undercover. We…uh…haven't talked yet," I heard myself stuttering.

Helen's head came up. "Oops. Sorry about that. I shouldn't have assumed." She spun around and headed for the door. "Guess you two need to talk. But I thought you'd want to know the baby's doing fine."

"What baby?" Joe's eyes were wide open.

I gulped. Here we go. No delaying this. I put my hand under

the covers and crossed my fingers. "The baby you and I are going to have sometime in late October or early November."

He leaned forward in his chair, face very close to mine. The light was back in his eyes. I took that as a good sign. He put his hand on my belly where Helen's scope had been. I took that as an even better sign.

He rose up halfway and kissed my forehead, then leaned down and put the side of his head on my belly for a long time, as if he was listening to the baby's heartbeat.

After a few moments, he sat back. He reached for my arm and began a slow stroking with his fingertips, just the tips of his fingers lightly going back and forth on the inside of my arm. It was something his mother used to do for him when he was a small child. She called it soothing. And it was.

I waited for him to speak.

After an eternity, his mouth opened. "I suppose if it's a girl, you're going to want to name her Sadie."

"Sadie's full name is Seraphim."

He gave me a long serious look, the tip of his tongue between his lips. "I'm not doing Seraphim."

He continued the delicate stroking on the inside of my arm. "Sadie Morgan will be a good name for a girl of ours."

Ours. Thank you, God.

I smiled and relaxed. "What if it's a boy?"

His turn to smile. "Well, then we both know what name we'll give a boy."

"Won't our dog be confused?"

"Probably."

Bourne Morris

Bourne Morris began writing at Bennington College where she studied under the late poet laureate, Howard Nemerov. After college, she worked at *McCall's* Magazine and then went to Ogilvy&Mather, New York during the "Mad Men" era. David Ogilvy and his colleagues treated her wonderfully, promoted her several times and then sent her west to become head of their agency in Los Angeles. She had a splendid run in advertising.

In 1983, she joined the University of Nevada Reno as a full professor in Journalism where she taught until 2009. She learned about campus politics when she served as chair of the faculty senate. She retired to write mysteries in 2009 after an equally wonderful teaching career.

The Red Solaris Mystery Series
by Bourne Morris

THE RED QUEEN'S RUN (#1)
THE RISE OF THE RED QUEEN (#2)
THE RED QUEEN RULES (#3)

Available at booksellers nationwide and online

Visit www.henerypress.com for details

Henery Press Mystery Books

And finally, before you go...
Here are a few other mysteries
you might enjoy:

TELL ME NO LIES

Lynn Chandler Willis

An Ava Logan Mystery (#1)

Ava Logan, single mother and small business owner, lives deep in the heart of the Appalachian Mountains, where poverty and pride reign. As publisher of the town newspaper, she's busy balancing election season stories and a rash of ginseng thieves.

And then the story gets personal. After her friend is murdered, Ava digs for the truth all the while juggling her two teenage children, her friend's orphaned toddler, and her own muddied past. Faced with threats against those closest to her, Ava must find the killer before she, or someone she loves, ends up dead.

Available at booksellers nationwide and online

Visit www.henerypress.com for details

WHEN LIES CRUMBLE
Alan Cupp

A Carter Mays Mystery (#1)

Chicago PI Carter Mays is thrust into a house of lies when local rich girl Cindy Bedford hires him. Turns out her fiancé failed to show up on their wedding day, the same day millions of dollars are stolen from her father's company. While Carter takes the case, Cindy's father tries to find him his own way. With nasty secrets, hidden finances, and a trail of revenge, it's soon apparent no one is who they say they are.

Carter searches for the truth, but the situation grows more volatile as panic collides with vulnerability. Broken relationships and blurred loyalties turn deadly, fueled by past offenses and present vendettas in a quest to reveal the truth behind the lies before no one, including Carter, gets out alive.

Available at booksellers nationwide and online

Visit www.henerypress.com for details

SHADOW OF DOUBT

Nancy Cole Silverman

A Carol Childs Mystery (#1)

When a top Hollywood Agent is found poisoned in the bathtub of her home suspicion quickly turns to one of her two nieces. But Carol Childs, a reporter for a local talk radio station doesn't believe it. The suspect is her neighbor and friend, and also her primary source for insider industry news. When a media frenzy pits one niece against the other—and the body count starts to rise—Carol knows she must save her friend from being tried in courts of public opinion.

But even the most seasoned reporter can be surprised, and when a Hollywood psychic shows up in Carol's studio one night and warns her there will be more deaths, things take an unexpected turn. Suddenly nobody is above suspicion. Carol must challenge both her friendship and the facts, and the only thing she knows for certain is the killer is still out there and the closer she gets to the truth, the more danger she's in.

Available at booksellers nationwide and online

Visit www.henerypress.com for details

www.ingramcontent.com/pod-product-compliance
Lightning Source LLC
Chambersburg PA
CBHW070449260626
47161CB00004B/1252